HIDDEN THREATS

Sandra Orchard

Annie's®
AnniesFiction.com

Books in the Sweet Intrigue series

Betrayal of Trust
Burning Danger
Christmas Peril
Dangerous at Heart
Web of Lies
Deceptive Truths
Fatal Waters
Gathering Storms
Under Suspicion
Guilty Secrets
Hidden Threats
Deadly Tides

Hidden Threats
Copyright © 2021, 2024 Annie's.

All rights reserved. No part of this publication may be reproduced, stored in a retrieval system, or transmitted in any form or by any means—electronic, mechanical, photocopying, recording or otherwise—without the prior written permission of the publisher. The only exception is brief quotations in printed reviews. For information address Annie's, 306 East Parr Road, Berne, Indiana 46711-1138.

The characters and events in this book are fictional, and any resemblance to actual persons or events is coincidental.

Library of Congress-in-Publication Data
Hidden Threats / by Sandra Orchard
p. cm.
ISBN: 978-1-64025-708-5
I. Title
2021941929

AnniesFiction.com
(800) 282-6643
Annie's Sweet Intrigue™
Series Creator: Shari Lohner
Editor: Lorie Jones

10 11 12 13 14 | Printed in China | 9 8 7 6 5 4 3 2

1

Police Officer Tom Olson had years of experience spotting a person of interest in a crowd. But nothing prepared him for the jolt of awareness he received when he zeroed in on his younger sister's new teacher, Miss Sound. The petite brunette greeting parents in the corner of the schoolyard was more attractive than he recalled from their first meeting at his neighbors' funeral.

Maybe Tom should cover Katy's transportation to and from school for his mom more often. Not that Katy couldn't ride the bus. His mom wasn't comfortable with the option, even though his eighteen-year-old sister with special needs had already been attending the K-12 charter school on Martha's Vineyard for the past five years.

Katy bounced from one foot to the other, eagerly scanning the crowd. "Do you see Miss Sound?"

"Yes." He pointed in the teacher's direction. "Over there."

Miss Sound swept a wayward strand of hair over her shoulder. With a warm smile, she shook the hand of Ian Culp, a solidly built, fair-haired young man and one of Katy's classmates.

"She looks so nice." Katy tugged Tom's uniform sleeve. "Come on. Let's go meet her."

Tom willingly obliged. When they got close enough, they heard the heated demands of Blake Culp, Ian's hulking father. By the sound of it, Ian hadn't scored a high enough grade last year to be permitted to play on the all-island football team, and his dad expected the new teacher to do something to fix the situation.

Ian toed the dirt, obviously embarrassed.

Not wanting to risk escalating the scene, Tom dragged his feet in hopes Blake would back off and take his request to the principal as Miss Sound suggested.

Ellen Donovan, one of the school's regular substitute teachers, stepped into Tom's path. "It's nice to see you again." The redhead wore an elegant dress and spiked heels. Her outfit was more suitable for a night on the town than to teach a class of students. She paused in front of him and used his arm to steady her balance, then scraped a clump of wet dirt from one of her heels. "After last night's rain, I should have known better than to wear these shoes for our opening day meet and greet."

Tom nodded, sparing her only a glance as Blake's voice grew more abrasive.

Ellen tracked the direction of his gaze. "I see you've spotted Rachel Sound, the school's newest hire. I imagine it'll be challenging for her adjusting to a new home and job with the tragic death of her in-laws still so fresh."

Tom winced. Miss Sound had moved into his neighbors' summer cottage following their tragic car accident a couple of months ago. He'd been so busy helping out at the camp in his free time that he hadn't made the effort to even introduce himself to his new next-door neighbor, let alone offer his condolences for her loss, aside from their brief encounter at the funeral.

With so few neighbors on their sparsely populated and densely wooded back road, Miss Sound probably would have appreciated knowing she could call on him in an emergency, especially now that the owners of the other two houses closest to her had moved back to the mainland for the winter.

"She's a widow with a boy named Jimmy," Ellen went on, fussing with her short, wind-ruffled hair. "I suppose the principal thought a single mother would be more reliable or determined to settle in for the long term. But personally, I don't see it. I've been covering classes for this place for three years, and I—"

"Excuse me," Tom interrupted, sensing the conversation was switching to gossip. He clasped his sister's hand to still her bouncing. "I need to introduce Katy to her new teacher so I can get to work."

"Of course," Ellen said. "I'm sure I'll see you around school. Someone always seems to be calling in sick."

Thankfully, Blake abandoned his quest to convince Miss Sound to bend the rules.

Tom realized he should be thinking of the widow as Mrs. Sound. He'd heard Katy refer to her as Miss Sound so often that it was stuck in his head, but he determined to change it.

Mrs. Sound turned and smiled at Katy. "Hello, there," the woman said brightly. "Are you one of my new students?"

His sister's grin stretched from ear to ear. "Yes, I'm Katy Olson. My mom says we're going to garden this year."

"That's right," Mrs. Sound responded. "Do you like to garden?"

"Oh yes!" Katy exclaimed. "I grew beans this summer. But isn't it too late to grow stuff now?"

"It is," Mrs. Sound agreed. "That's why I went ahead and started our class garden this past summer. But there's still a lot we can do before winter sets in."

Katy squealed. "Can I see the garden? Do you have beans too?"

"You bet," Mrs. Sound replied. "I can take you now if you and your dad have time."

Katy giggled.

"Mrs. Sound, I'm her brother, Tom Olson. Our dad's gone."

"I'm sorry." The light in the teacher's eyes dimmed.

Tom immediately regretted the last part. "It was a long time ago," he added, sensing that the poor woman's thoughts had scattered at the unexpected revelation, no doubt revisiting her own recent loss.

"Please call me Rachel."

He nodded, glad to be able to think of her by a reference other than Mrs. Sound or Katy's teacher. The name suited her. Rachel was the name of the favored wife of Jacob—beautiful in form and countenance. "I'd like to see the garden."

"Right this way." Rachel motioned toward a small plowed patch beyond a copse of trees. "I love the school's multiage, project-based paradigm," she rushed on, as if feeling the need to fill the silence. "I have so many ideas to study math by counting, weighing, and preserving the harvest, then comparing it to what I planted and planning how much we'd need to plant next year to get a desired outcome. Also, the opportunities to cover scientific concepts are vast—from botany to etymology to geology, even chemistry with fertilizers and such. And I've chosen an array of literature and poetry centered on the theme."

Tom grinned. "Let me guess. *The Secret Garden*."

"Absolutely." Rachel chuckled.

Her laughter was contagious. He was glad Rachel was his sister's teacher.

Rachel's abrupt halt and horrified gasp sliced through his bemused thoughts.

"What is it?" Tom asked, his senses on high alert.

"It's ruined," Rachel announced, her voice on the verge of tears.

She was right. Stakes were tossed willy-nilly about the garden plot, and pieces of string that had likely marked rows had been yanked up, mangling more than a few plants in the process.

Rachel's next step was as wobbly as her voice. "Why would someone do this?"

Noticing telltale holes throughout the patch, Tom knelt down to make a closer examination. "I would guess that someone wearing spiked heels might be your culprit." He pointed to one of the holes.

"No." Rachel retrieved an uprooted stake and placed it back in the hole. "Those are from where the stakes were. I'm sure it was only kids being kids. Maybe they didn't realize it was set up to be used for a school project." She frowned. "Or it was meant to be a prank on the new teacher."

He stood, not entirely convinced of the theory, not with Ellen's muddy spiked heel fresh in his memory. But would she have been bold enough to tromp through the garden in plain sight of half the school? He glanced over his shoulder, but the trees shielded the garden plot from view of the playing fields where students, faculty, and parents milled about.

Katy hugged herself and shook her head. "A bad person did this."

"It's okay," Rachel assured her. "I can still make it work somehow."

"I can give you a hand fixing it," Tom volunteered.

"I appreciate the offer, but doing it myself will probably be quicker," Rachel said. "I think the damage looks worse than it really is. Once I get the stakes back in place, it won't take long to restring my grids." She gave them both a warm smile. "While I do that, how about you take Katy to see the cool project our art teacher has set up for students to do today?"

"If you're sure," he said.

"I'm sure," Rachel insisted.

As Tom steered Katy toward the rest of the opening day festivities, she kicked a crumpled paper ball.

"What do we have here?" He stooped down and gingerly unfolded the mud-streaked paper—the kind of lined paper found in the spiral-bound notebooks students were encouraged to purchase for their classes. "It's someone's exercise program." *Maybe a football player's.* He flipped the paper so Rachel could see.

"I doubt it's connected to the vandalism," she said.

"Does Blake Culp have a beef with you?" Tom asked.

"No," Rachel said, sounding shocked by the suggestion. "He was merely hoping I might be able to provide his son with supplemental work so Principal Sutton would waive the playing prohibition placed on Ian." She shook her head. "I'm sorry. I shouldn't be discussing other students with you."

"No need to apologize," he said. "Blake was bellowing loud enough for half the school to hear. You haven't betrayed any private information he didn't broadcast himself."

"Still . . ." Rachel let her voice trail off and avoided his gaze.

Her obvious contrition made Tom like her all the more. Rachel was nothing like Ellen. He imagined the substitute teacher would have jumped on the opportunity to gossip about Blake and Ian. Remembering Ellen's muddy shoe, he replayed their conversation in his head. Despite the seemingly concerned things she'd said about the school's newest teacher, there had been an underlying note of resentment. Clearly, Ellen had expected to score the permanent teaching post over a newcomer to the island.

Tom opened his mouth to ask Rachel about her interactions with Ellen, but then he thought better of it. There was no need to raise suspicions that might turn out to be unwarranted.

Instead, he asked her a question that was more general. "Has anyone expressed hostility toward you since you moved to the island?"

She hesitated before answering. "No."

After saying goodbye to Rachel, Tom prodded Katy toward the art tent and searched the crowd for Ellen. They needed to have another chat—this one in private.

Rachel tucked her precocious six-year-old son into bed. "Do you like your new school?"

"Yeah, Billy is in my class," Jimmy answered.

"That's great," she told him. Billy was a friend he'd made since moving to the island after her in-laws' deaths.

He frowned. "But I wish Grandma and Grandpa were still here."

"Me too," Rachel said with a sigh. Never mind that she and Jimmy wouldn't have this lovely home to live in or a new job and life on the island. Jimmy had already lost too much in his young life between his grandparents' accident and his father's brain aneurysm three years before. She pressed a kiss to the top of her son's head. "Good night." She switched off his bedside lamp and closed the door.

Rachel made herself a cup of cocoa, then settled in at her desk on the main floor to work on the next day's lesson plans. Enough of the plants had been unaffected by the prankster that she could still go ahead with the lesson on how to calculate yields per square yard with reasonable accuracy and then extrapolate the information to calculate yields per acre. In future lessons, she planned to have the students use the information to calculate what it would cost to grow various types of produce. She also wanted them to explore the many variables that were involved—from the cost of the seed to labor.

For a little while, she brainstormed a list of other math problems she could present to the students based on their harvest yields versus the number of seeds planted and the space needed to grow the plants.

Setting down her pen, Rachel powered on her computer. While she waited for the screen to come to life, she sat back in her desk chair and sipped her cocoa. Skimming the student names on her class list, she conjured up a mental image of each one.

When she reached Katy Olson's name, her lips curved into a smile. The girl was sweet and incredibly bright. Rachel had struggled to understand her speech at first, since she spoke so quickly in her excitement. But before long, Rachel had realized Katy's understanding far surpassed her language skills. In fact, unlike the average child with Down syndrome who tended to peak at a mental age of eight or nine, Rachel suspected Katy's mental age was comparable to an eleven-year-old's.

Rachel assumed that Katy's older brother had a lot to do with her impressive development. Tom obviously adored his sister and no doubt spent a good deal of time helping her gain her independence. He seemed like the kind of guy anyone would be lucky to have on their side.

Her smile widened at the memory of his embarrassed expression when she mistook him for Katy's dad. She must have been distracted by Blake Culp's confrontation to make such a blunder. Tom certainly didn't appear old enough to be the father of a high school senior. He had thick brown hair, a rugged beard untouched by gray, and an athletic build.

Her computer's home screen appeared on the monitor—an image she'd taken of the garden last week before the vandalism. Thank goodness Tom and Katy had been with her when she discovered the damage. Rachel had been on edge after speaking with Blake, and she wasn't sure how she would have coped if she hadn't felt compelled to hold herself together for Katy's sake.

Tom's concern and offer of assistance had felt especially nice too. Not that she wasn't used to handling major crises. But before now, there had always been someone she could lean on. When she was a teenager, James had been there for her when she lost her parents. She'd eventually married him, and his parents had been there for her when she lost him. Since their death two months ago, she'd truly been flying solo, and worse than that, she'd been dodging attacks from the last place she'd expected—her brother-in-law. Richard Sound was her late husband's twin brother, and he had become as big a bully as Blake had been this morning. Maybe that was why Tom's kindness had felt like such a sweet balm.

Rachel skimmed the names on her student list once more, but she couldn't begin to guess which one might have been responsible for the damage. She wasn't surprised that some kids had decided to prank her. New teachers were often a target for such mischief. Thankfully, the prank hadn't been particularly malicious, given that most of the damage was easy enough to undo.

Car lights flickered past the window. Perhaps Tom was returning home from his shift. Knowing she had a police officer living close by was reassuring. Her mother-in-law had mentioned as much when they bought the place. But Rachel had forgotten, since she'd never had the opportunity to meet Tom until the funeral, and he hadn't been in uniform when he introduced himself to her.

Forcing thoughts of her handsome neighbor from her mind, Rachel focused on the lesson plans she'd typed up for the week. Her stomach still felt as jumbled as it had this morning—a symptom of the first week jitters she endured every year. She wondered how her new students would be and what challenges they would encounter.

"The plan is good, and the students will enjoy the activities," she said aloud and shut down the computer.

Sleep was what she needed more than anything. Rachel checked the lock on the door, flicked off all the lights on the main floor, and headed upstairs to bed.

Within minutes, she drifted off to sleep to the sound of the wind whistling in the eaves. She dreamed of picking beans with her students, which morphed into climbing a giant beanstalk into the clouds with Jimmy.

A loud noise jerked her awake. Rachel jackknifed to a sitting position and squinted at the sudden brightness. Why were the lights on? Her gaze shot to the window. The sky was still black.

Her heart thudded as voices disturbed the silence. They sounded as if they were coming from downstairs.

Jimmy screamed.

Rachel sprang out of bed and dashed toward his room. Lights lit her way—lights she remembered switching off before going to bed.

Someone was inside her house.

Yawning, Tom steered onto the dirt road that led to his house. His shift should have ended three hours ago, but he hadn't been about to walk away from his last call without doing everything he could. It had been a domestic disturbance, and the fear in the eyes of the woman who answered the door was unmistakable. He reached down to turn off his police radio, but he stopped at the mention of his street.

The dispatcher repeated the address for the home invasion.

Rachel's place.

Tom stepped on the gas and radioed the dispatcher. "I'm a minute from the scene. Please send backup." He was driving his own vehicle, so he didn't have a siren to reassure the single mother and son that help was on the way, but the element of surprise might help him catch the intruder.

When he arrived, he resisted the urge to swerve into her driveway. Instead, he parked his truck diagonally across the exit.

All the lights in the house seemed to be on. Tom stole through the trees along the driveway. The curtains were open on the main floor, affording him a clear view of every room, except the bathroom and laundry room. The TV blared, but there was no sign of an intruder or Rachel. Tom peered up at the second-story windows and slowly rounded the house. The lights were on in every room upstairs too, but the curtains were all closed.

The curtain in a room at the back of the house shifted.

Was the little family hiding in there? Or was the intruder holding them captive?

He relayed the situation to the dispatcher.

"Backup is fifteen minutes out," the dispatcher reported.

"This family might not have fifteen minutes," Tom said. "Does the 911 operator still have the homeowner on the phone?"

After a long pause, the dispatcher answered in the affirmative.

His galloping pulse slowed to a canter. If Rachel was still on the phone, then the intruder wasn't threatening her. "Have the dispatcher tell her I'm outside and to open the window of the bedroom she's in."

A moment later, the curtain edged aside, and his frightened neighbor's face appeared.

Tom stepped into view and waved.

Rachel opened the window. "Tom, is that you?" she hissed, scarcely louder than a whisper.

"Yes," he said. "Are you okay?"

"No. Someone's in our house."

Tom immediately receded from the light pooled on the ground from the first-floor windows. "Have you seen how many?"

"No, but they were inside while we were asleep," Rachel answered. "They left every light on. I don't know how I slept through it."

"I think they're gone now," he assured her. "There's no vehicle out here, and I can't see anyone on the main floor unless he's holed up in the bathroom or laundry room. If you come down and let me in, I can do a sweep of the house for you."

She shook her head vigorously. "I can't leave Jimmy alone. And I won't risk taking him downstairs until I know for sure no one's there. Break in if you have to."

"Sit tight." Tom circled the house once more, peeking through the windows into all the corners of the rooms he could see. Satisfied no one was waiting to ambush him, he inspected the doors. Both had simple locks in the door handle and no dead bolts, but neither door appeared to have been tampered with.

Tom breached the back door in less than a minute. It opened into the laundry room. He checked the closet and the bathroom. Both were clear. He worked his way around the main floor, checking every possible hiding place. Finding the TV remote, he clicked it off and listened.

There was no sound of breathing. No sound of footsteps. No squeaks of floorboards.

Staying close to the wall, Tom climbed the stairs and scanned the hallway, then systematically cleared each room, leaving the bedroom where the family was hiding for last. Not wanting to frighten Rachel, he tapped on the door. "It's Officer Tom Olson. May I come in?"

"Yes."

Aware her intruder could yet be inside the room, ready to trap him, Tom pushed the door open slowly.

Rachel sat in a rocking chair next to the window with her sleeping son folded in her arms.

Tom nodded to her, but he checked behind the closed closet door before announcing, "The house is clear."

She exhaled.

Tom clicked the radio that was pinned to his shoulder and told the dispatcher to cancel the backup. He would stick around as long as it took to gather evidence to catch the creep who'd terrorized a poor widow and ensure she felt safe. The last thing Rachel needed now was a bunch of cops she didn't know parading through the house and grilling her.

Tom jutted his chin toward her sleeping son. "Would you like me to carry him to his bed for you?"

"Yes, thank you." The tremble in her voice tugged at his heart.

He gently lifted Jimmy from her arms and inhaled the sweet lavender scent that clung to the child—his mother's scent.

Rachel followed Tom to the bed and tucked the sheets lovingly around the boy, then pressed a kiss to his forehead. Jimmy didn't even stir. She must have done a convincing acting job to make him feel safe despite her own fears.

Tom's admiration for Rachel kicked up another couple of notches. "Perhaps we could talk downstairs," he whispered. "I need to take your statement and have you check to see if anything's been stolen. Then I'll dust for fingerprints."

"Right." She glanced down at her nightclothes, and a blush bloomed on her cheeks. "Let me change first."

She was wearing shorts and a T-shirt, nothing to be embarrassed about on an island where the beaches were packed with bikini-clad sunbathers all summer, but he respected her modesty.

"Of course." He stepped out of Jimmy's room. "I need to grab some stuff from the truck. I'll meet you down there when you're ready."

While outside Tom examined the ground around the doors and the first-floor windows with his high-powered flashlight, trying to determine how the intruder had broken in and left.

When he returned to the house, Rachel was in the kitchen, filling the kettle with water. "Would you like a cup of tea?" she asked. "I have herbals if you don't want caffeine."

"Sure, a mint tea or whatever you're having would be great."

"Mint it is." She retrieved a box of tea from the cupboard.

Tom sat down at the kitchen table and opened his notebook. Soon the aroma of peppermint filled the kitchen, helping—he hoped—to make her home feel a little more like the haven it should. "Have you had a chance to see if anything's been taken?"

Rachel swallowed audibly, and the teacup rattled as she set it on its saucer. "Nothing seems to be missing. I don't own anything very valuable. I don't have any expensive jewelry, and I don't keep cash in the house. The computer is a few years old, and the TV is even older. Both are still here."

Tom noted her answer, which further validated his theory. "Does anyone else have a key to the place?"

"As far as I know, no one on the island has a key to the house. But my brother-in-law in Boston likely does." She fiddled with a second teacup. "Another good reason to change the locks."

"I'd recommend adding dead bolts," he said. "They're more secure."

Rachel lifted the whistling kettle and poured the water into a teapot. "I thought Martha's Vineyard was supposed to be the kind of place where people didn't even bother to lock their doors. That's what my mother-in-law used to say when we visited in the summers."

"It's true," Tom admitted. "A lot of people don't feel it's necessary, but one never knows when an opportunist might take advantage of a situation."

She rounded the counter and busied herself preparing the cups of tea. "I understand that. But there's something abnormal about breaking into my house to leave on all the lights and the TV."

"It's definitely unusual," he agreed, accepting the cup of tea she offered him. "I couldn't find any suspicious footprints around the doors or windows, and none appeared to have been breached."

Rachel slumped into the chair opposite him. "Well, he got inside somehow."

Tom opened his fingerprint kit. "Apparently, he wanted us to believe he touched every light switch in the place." He dusted the light switch over the kitchen sink—one an intruder wasn't likely to think of, yet it had been on when Tom arrived and still was. The switch had no fingerprints on it. "Did you clean this switch since coming downstairs?"

"No, I wiped it after doing the dishes at suppertime, because I splashed spaghetti sauce on it."

"Is there any other switch that controls this light?" he asked.

"No, I don't think so," she replied. "Are you saying the intruder wore gloves? That we can't even get a fingerprint to ID him?"

"I'm thinking the situation might actually be less sinister than you think."

Rachel raised her eyebrows. "What do you mean?"

"I see your home is equipped with a smart system," Tom said. "Do you control it with an app on your phone?"

"No, I've never installed the app on my phone," she said. "I don't even use the system."

"In that case, I'd recommend disabling the box," he responded. "As an extra measure of protection, I'd keep your home's Wi-Fi off when you're not using it."

"Are you saying you don't think someone came into the house?" Rachel asked, sounding shocked. "You think they hacked into my Wi-Fi?"

Tom nodded, but that scenario hadn't been his first thought. "I was considering your son."

"Jimmy woke up screaming. There's no way he toddled downstairs seconds before that and turned on everything in the house to scare me, then raced back upstairs before the lights came on."

He chuckled. "I agree, but earlier in the evening he might have somehow opened the app that controls your system and unknowingly changed the program settings."

Rachel glanced at the desk in the corner. "I did let him play an educational game on his grandparents' old desktop computer while I was preparing supper. Maybe he got into the system's program then." Her shoulders seemed to melt as if the tension of the past hour were draining out of them. "Do you really think a six-year-old could have caused all this?"

"The fact that everything controlled by the system came on at once makes me think that's the most likely explanation," Tom replied. "With one click, your son could have selected an option that covered the entire system. Whereas if someone hacked in to try to harass you, he probably would have toyed with you by intermittently flipping things on and off."

"I see what you mean," she said. "Or it could have been another prank. There are some bright students at school. I wouldn't be surprised if they were capable of hacking into my Wi-Fi."

Tom mentally replayed his conversation with Ellen about the vandalism to the school garden. Although she'd claimed she never touched the garden, she'd betrayed more than a hint of animosity toward Rachel, probably over the fact she'd lost the full-time placement to her. But while Ellen struck him as the type of person who might lash out, he doubted her reaction would be this calculated or that she'd have the knowledge to pull off the scheme. A student hacker seemed more plausible. "I can ask our department's tech guy if he can get into your system and trace the origin of the commands."

"I'd appreciate it." Rachel sipped her tea.

Tom was encouraged to see that her hands no longer trembled. Perhaps she would be able to get some more sleep after all. "Well, there's not much else I can do." He drained his tea, then scribbled his cell number on the back of his business card and set the card on the table. "Don't hesitate to call me if you notice something suspicious going on. And let me know if you remember anything else that might be helpful in uncovering what happened."

"I will," she said, picking up the card and studying its details. "Thank you."

He ignored the reflexive response to say he was simply doing his job. "You're welcome." As odd as it seemed, considering he'd only recently met Rachel, he didn't want her to think his helping her was just the job. He wanted her to know he genuinely cared. He gently covered her hand with his own. Her soft, cool skin warmed beneath his touch. "I can be here in under two minutes if you need help."

A trembling smile lifted the corners of her lips, and her eyes filled as she nodded.

Tom quickly withdrew his hand and carried his teacup to the kitchen sink. "Do you know how to disable your Wi-Fi?"

Rachel sprang up, reached around the desk, and tugged a cord from the wall. "Off."

"Good. I've already checked that all the locks on the windows are secure. I'll lock the door as I leave."

After thanking him again, she walked him to the door. The porch light stayed on until he opened the door of his truck.

"Sleep well," he whispered into the night.

During afternoon recess on Friday, Rachel scrambled to find the portable bulletin board she'd prepared for her last class of the day. For the third time, she returned to the corner where she was sure she'd left it and thumbed through the poster boards leaning against the wall.

The custodian poked his head inside her classroom. Jack Drew was a slim older man. "Can I help you find something?" he asked in a kind voice.

"I hope so," Rachel said. "Have you seen anyone with a bulletin board?"

"Nope," he said. "But if you need one, I can show you where we store them in the supply closet."

"Thanks, but that's okay," she said. "I know where they're stored. The one I'm missing already has today's lesson pinned to it."

"You might want to check the closet anyway," Jack suggested. "If someone found the board, they would have put it in there."

"I will." Rachel glanced at the clock. Recess would be over in five minutes. If the bulletin board wasn't in the supply closet, she'd have to take a whiteboard and write out the lesson from memory, without the benefit of the illustrations she'd printed. There was a large bulletin board mounted on her classroom wall, but she didn't want to use it. She planned to teach the lesson outside, so the students could take measurements as they went along.

She gritted her teeth as she stalked down the hall to the supply closet inside the staff's break room. She'd hoped the prank-the-new-teacher streak had ended with the wrecked garden and the midnight shenanigans, which Tom's tech guy confirmed had been triggered by someone who'd accessed her smart system's app remotely. Unfortunately, he hadn't been able to pinpoint the culprit's location.

Rachel greeted the two staff members sipping coffee in the break room, then rummaged through the supply closet. She didn't mean to eavesdrop, but the substitute teacher who'd introduced herself on opening day as Ellen Donovan spoke too loudly to ignore.

"If I'm going to make my final property tax installment, I might have to take a second job," Ellen confided to the other teacher.

Rachel flinched. When were property taxes due? She couldn't recall seeing a bill and made a mental note to check. Getting in arrears with any payments connected to the house was the kind of thing Richard might use against her.

At the sound of the recess bell, Rachel grabbed a portable whiteboard and a pack of markers. She'd have to make do with them.

Her students had already taken their seats in the classroom by the time Rachel returned.

"Since the bulletin board I prepared for this afternoon's lesson seems to have sprouted legs and walked away..." Rachel paused, hoping a snicker or a blush might betray the culprit, but not one person so much as twitched. "We'll have to manage with this." She raised the portable whiteboard. "And you'll have to look up the illustrations yourselves when you do the assignment."

A collective groan confirmed they understood her point—the prank was on them, since they would have more work to do because of it. But still, no one accused anyone else, let alone confessed.

Rachel studied each student's face. Ian didn't seem to be paying much attention, which had been his status quo all week. It wasn't exactly the attitude she expected from someone hoping she'd waive his probation. Of all her students, she figured he carried the most resentment toward her because she hadn't immediately surrendered to his father's demands.

She led her students to the garden and conducted the lesson as best she could without her prepared materials. Despite the earlier damage to the garden, she'd managed to proceed with all her lessons exactly as she'd planned them until today.

As the students settled into gathering measurements and drawing their diagrams, Rachel's thoughts wandered to Tom's question on the first day of school. He'd asked her if anyone had expressed hostility toward her since moving to Martha's Vineyard.

At the time, she'd immediately thought of her brother-in-law. Richard was her late husband's twin, but the similarities between them ended with their physical appearance. James had been caring and selfless, and his brother was utterly self-centered. From the beginning, Richard had hated that his parents had invited Rachel to live with them in Boston after James's death and then to vacation with them on the island in the summers. He even opposed his mother babysitting Jimmy so Rachel could return to her teaching position to help with the bills. Was it any wonder that Richard had cried foul when they learned his parents had left her their summer cottage?

Was Richard behind the vandalism and the hacking into the cottage's smart system? She wouldn't put it past him to resort to such tactics to get her to move.

The will stipulated that she had to live in the cottage as her primary residence year-round for at least two years. Otherwise, it would be sold, and the proceeds returned to the estate for distribution. The lawyer had said that Rachel's in-laws had recently added the allocation and condition to the will, no doubt after learning she'd been offered a teaching position on the island. She'd only accepted the offer after they said she could use their cottage through the school year. Now that she'd quit her position in Boston and accepted the Martha's Vineyard posting, losing the home wasn't an option she could afford, and Richard knew it.

Even so, Rachel certainly hadn't wanted to talk about her family issues with Tom, cop or not. And at the time, the vandalism had seemed far more likely to be the work of a student. It still did. She couldn't picture Richard in his expensive tailored suit yanking up stakes in the school's garden. How would he even have known it was a project for her class?

Unless Richard had hired someone to spy on her. She shivered. Now she was letting her imagination get the best of her. But she probably should pay more attention to her surroundings to be safe. Sensing she was being watched at that very moment, she glanced over her shoulder.

Tom, especially handsome in his dark-blue uniform, strode across the soccer field toward her. How had she not noticed until now how vivid his blue eyes were? They weren't pale like the sky. They were dark sapphire like Jimmy's most treasured sea glass find.

Rachel had been so relieved when Tom showed up at her house Tuesday night mere minutes after her 911 call. She'd feared help would be at least twenty minutes away. But then Tom had arrived like a knight in shining armor in the moonlight, ready to slay her dragons.

She laughed at the silly thought. She'd clearly been watching too many fantasy movies with Jimmy. Tom was here to pick up his sister, as he'd done every afternoon this week. As he'd also done every afternoon, he motioned Rachel aside and quietly asked if she'd had any more trouble.

Touched by his ongoing concern, she shifted her gaze from his to the windows of her classroom across the schoolyard. "Not unless you count a missing bulletin board. I'm sure it was another prank on the new teacher."

He nodded. "Has the locksmith installed dead bolts on your doors yet?"

"Not yet. We've been playing telephone tag all week."

"I can come over and install them this evening," Tom offered.

"I don't want to bother you," Rachel said. "I'm sure you have more than enough on your plate without adding my to-do list."

"Not at all. I'll sleep better knowing your home is secure."

Her heart started pounding. Worry for her kept him awake at night? What was he worried might happen? Once his tech guy confirmed the lights coming on in the middle of the night wasn't the work of Jimmy messing around on his grandparents' old computer, Tom had convinced her that a savvy student must have pulled the prank. Had he changed his mind?

"Is there something you're not telling me about Tuesday night's incident?" she asked.

"Of course not," he said.

But he said it too quickly. And in Rachel's experience, that usually meant someone was lying.

As Rachel drove to the post office after school, she did her best to maintain a lively conversation with her son in the back seat. But her disquieting conversation with Tom kept creeping into her thoughts.

Tom had been so insistent about installing the dead bolts. There had to be something he wasn't telling her. He'd claimed there wasn't, and she didn't truly know him well enough to read him. He seemed as if he were simply concerned for her well-being. But why was he concerned if he thought the incidents were harmless pranks?

"Here we are," she announced, interrupting Jimmy's story about playing with Billy at recess.

Jimmy clambered from the car, and they checked their post office box. It was empty again.

Rachel clasped Jimmy's hand and went to the counter to speak to the clerk. "I'm wondering if there's been a mix-up with my post office box number."

"What's the matter?" the woman asked.

"Besides my credit card bill last week and a couple of greeting cards when I first moved here almost two months ago, I haven't received any mail in weeks," Rachel explained. "I should have received an electricity bill and perhaps a property tax bill by now. Do you know when they come out?"

"They'll be delivered shortly," the clerk said. "Let me verify your address. Can I have your name?"

Rachel recited her name and address and the number of the post office box to which she had a key.

"Oh, you must be the Sounds' daughter-in-law," the woman said with kindness in her tone. "I'm so sorry for your loss."

"Thank you."

"Are the household bills still in your in-laws' names?" the clerk asked.

"I don't know," Rachel admitted. "I guess they might be."

"Well, that would explain the lack of mail. All their mail is forwarded to the executor of their will in Boston."

Rachel stifled a sigh. That meant their mail was sent to Richard. "I'll have to speak to him." She dreaded that conversation.

"Don't worry," the clerk said, obviously sensing her distress. "The executor is responsible for paying the property tax and any other bills from the estate until it's settled. I'm sure you won't suddenly find your electricity turned off or anything."

Rachel thanked the woman, then led Jimmy back to their car. Lately she wasn't sure about anything where her brother-in-law was concerned. She wouldn't be surprised if Richard ignored the bills and somehow held the past due notices against her.

"Can I watch TV at home?" Jimmy asked.

"For a little while," Rachel conceded. She usually avoided allowing him to fritter away his time in front of a screen when he could be playing, but it would distract him while she made the call. She didn't want Jimmy to overhear her conversation with his uncle.

When they got home, she fixed him a snack to tide him over until dinner. She powered up the Wi-Fi and found an educational show on the Internet.

Jimmy sat down in front of the TV with his snack.

After a fortifying breath, Rachel started to dial Richard's number, then changed her mind and phoned her lawyer, Lauren Witmer, instead.

"I have good news," Lauren said the moment she answered. "The judge has advised your brother-in-law not to waste his time and money contesting his parents' will."

"Will he listen?" Rachel asked. Since Richard was an attorney, it didn't really cost him anything to continue making her life miserable.

"According to the paperwork that came in today, you are officially entitled to continue living in the cottage," Lauren responded. "Richard can only demand the property be forfeited and sold if you leave. This should finally put an end to his harassment."

"That would be nice," Rachel said, but somehow she didn't feel as confident as her lawyer. Rachel asked about the house bills—bills that for all she knew Richard could be ignoring.

Lauren promised to find out if they could change the accounts to Rachel's name so there would be no chance of his pulling something underhanded.

After disconnecting the call, Rachel checked on Jimmy. He seemed to be enjoying the show, so she began chopping vegetables for supper.

Rachel couldn't understand her brother-in-law's animosity. She found it difficult to believe it was about the money. After all, Richard was a successful attorney. He'd already received the proceeds of his parents' primary residence in Boston, so he was hardly in need of the money from the sale of the cottage. Moreover, now that both his parents and his brother were gone, Jimmy was his last living relative. Rachel thought Richard would be more interested in spending time with his nephew than shutting him out of his life.

Did Richard blame her for his parents' deaths?

Rachel had overheard one of Richard's associates at the funeral speculate that she was cursed. She shivered. Was it any wonder? Every person she'd ever loved, save for Jimmy, had died tragically—first her parents, then her husband, and now his parents.

Some days it was all she could do to suppress her fear that Jimmy would be next.

When Rachel didn't answer her doorbell, Tom peeked through the living room's picture window. Her son was watching TV, and light spilled through the kitchen doorway. Assuming Rachel was preparing dinner, Tom debated whether to return in an hour after they'd finished eating. But by then the sun would be setting. Carrying his toolbox, he rounded the house and knocked on the back door.

A metal pan clattered.

Tom knocked on the door again. "It's Tom. Everything okay?"

"Yes, come in," Rachel called out.

He opened the door and entered the kitchen.

She picked up the fallen pan from the floor and took it to the sink. "My mind was a million miles away, and your knock made me jump."

"I'm sorry." Tom searched her eyes. Her response had been nonchalant, but he sensed an undercurrent of tension that hadn't been there this afternoon. "I can come back later if this isn't a good time."

"No, it's perfect," Rachel said. "You can stay for supper."

"You don't have to do that."

"I want you to join us," she insisted. "If you don't already have other plans. And if you like chicken."

He grinned. "I love chicken, and it tastes so much better when I don't have to cook it myself."

Her laughter chased away the cloud that had seemed to hover over her.

"And I don't have plans," Tom added. "Thank you."

Rachel's smile grew shy.

Suddenly, he felt awkward, so he hitched his thumb toward the door he'd just entered. "I'll start on this one first."

"Thanks," she said. "Let me know if you need anything."

Tom proceeded to drill out the door and set the dead bolt in place. He should recommend that Rachel have blocking inserted behind the doorjamb for reinforcement so a criminal couldn't simply pry the doorjamb back with a crowbar. He would have done it now, but he would have had to remove the drywall, and he wasn't prepared for that.

By the time he was finished with the back door, mouthwatering aromas made his stomach growl in anticipation. "Do I have time to do the front door before dinner?"

"It'll be about twenty minutes," she said.

"That should do it." Tom went outside and walked to the front door, so he wouldn't track dirt through the house. The front door was unlocked, and he made quick work of installing the dead bolt.

But as he started on the doorjamb, water blasted his back. "What in the world?" He spun around, but no one was there. A rotating sprinkler head in the front lawn had switched on. He dodged the spray to reach the outdoor tap and shut it off, but that didn't stop the sprinkler.

Drenched from the effort, Tom rushed into the kitchen.

Rachel gasped at his dripping clothes. "What happened?"

"Your sprinkler's blasting the porch, and I can't shut it off."

"That's weird. It's on a timer, but it's never soaked the porch before." Rachel furrowed her brow. "I turned the Wi-Fi on when I got home. It was the first time it's been on since Tuesday night. Maybe the hacker overrode the settings." She hurried to her computer and found the app that controlled the system. "Or can I disable the Wi-Fi? Will that stop it?"

"It might," he answered. "Or it might leave it on so that it doesn't get the stop message."

"I hate this system," she muttered.

A sudden noise made them jump. Water blasted the front window and sprayed through the open screen.

Tom slammed the window shut.

"It shouldn't reach that far." Rachel returned her attention to the computer. "There."

The fountain of water slowed to a trickle.

"I'll finish the door," he said, "then examine the spigot to see if I can figure out why it's shooting toward the window."

"While you're doing that, I'll pull the plug on the Wi-Fi, so you don't have to worry about getting another unexpected shower."

Tom chuckled. The twinkle in her eye had almost made the soaking worth it. He finished reinforcing the doorjamb without further incident and packed his tools in his now-damp toolbox. Then he walked over and inspected the in-ground watering system.

"What are you doing?" Rachel asked from the doorway.

He gave the fitting on the water spigot one final twist. "Adjusting the spigot so that it waters your garden instead of your house." Climbing to his feet, he debated whether or not to admit that he'd found three of the spigots facing the house when they shouldn't have been. He didn't want to add to her distress. The misdirected spigots might have been the result of incorrect installations, but he doubted that was the case. He had a bad feeling someone had recently moved them.

Was it another schoolboy prank?

Tossing his wrench into his toolbox, Tom grimaced. Messing with the school garden or hiding a bulletin board was one thing. But terrorizing the teacher by manipulating her home's smart system and moving spigots so they could potentially cause property damage was a whole different level of malice. How would her students even know where she lived?

Had someone looked her up online? Or followed her home from school?

Except what if the culprit wasn't a student? Tom clenched his jaw. Dealing with a stalker Rachel could identify was challenging enough. How was he supposed to protect her from a nameless, faceless perpetrator?

The next afternoon, after cleaning their small cottage and catching up on laundry, Rachel got out coloring books, modeling clay, and puzzles to keep Jimmy occupied while she prepared the following week's lessons.

Her son plopped down on the floor in the living room and began coloring.

She spread her notes on the kitchen table. Maybe if she saw all her ideas at once it would help her organize them into a cohesive plan. But her mind kept wandering to the strange conversation she'd had with Tom over the previous night's dinner. Or perhaps *strained* would be a better description.

He'd asked if she'd mentioned where she lived to her class, and she had said that she hadn't. Then he'd asked if she'd had anyone over to do house or yard maintenance recently, which she hadn't. He'd seemed to want to ask more questions, but she'd sensed he had been reluctant to do so in front of Jimmy.

"This isn't the first school where students have played pranks on me," Rachel had told Tom with a wink at Jimmy.

Her son had taken great pleasure in recounting for Tom the story of the frog that hopped out of her desk drawer on her first day of school one year—a story his grandfather had told often.

Tom's laughter had seemed forced.

Thankfully, Jimmy hadn't seemed to have noticed. He'd returned to his show the instant he'd finished his dinner.

But the absence of her little one's ears hadn't eased Tom's reticence. When Rachel had finally coaxed him to share what was on his mind, she'd almost wished she hadn't. He'd asked if she'd ever been bothered by a stalker.

She couldn't believe it. A stalker was the last thing she'd imagined having to contend with on the idyllic island.

Rachel hadn't been here long enough to make any enemies. Blake had been angry that she'd refused to reverse the decision to keep his son from playing football, but the garden was trashed before they'd even discussed the matter. And surely, he couldn't imagine that hacking into her home's smart system would help his cause.

Her brother-in-law was the only person who had a vested interest in making her too frightened to stay in the house. She'd resisted admitting to Richard's animosity. Somehow doing so seemed like a slight on her in-laws. After all, Richard was their son. And the last thing she wanted to do was wrongfully slander their son.

"Miss Sound," Katy called through the kitchen's screen door.

Rachel opened the door and did a double take at the trays of unbaked pastries Katy and her brother held. "What's going on?"

"We ran out of room in Tom's oven," Katy said.

"We're making tarts for the Grandparents' Day celebration our church is hosting tomorrow afternoon," Tom explained. "We got carried away and made too many. I'm afraid we won't have enough time to bake them before my evening shift starts, so I was hoping we could borrow your oven."

"Bring them in," Rachel said, holding the door open. "Do you need the oven at 350?"

"Yes, thank you," he said.

"No problem." Rachel took the tray from Katy and put it on the counter, then set the oven to preheat. "They look like they're going to be delicious."

"They need to cook for twenty minutes." Tom set his tray on the stove.

A man who bakes—be still my fluttering heart. Rachel hid a smile. "No problem. I can bring them over when they're done."

"Are you sure you don't mind?" he asked.

"Of course not." Rachel grinned. "But I can't guarantee that one or two won't go missing."

Tom laughed. "Please feel free to help yourself. Once the aroma fills your kitchen, they are hard to resist. I can attest to that." His eyes twinkled, without a hint of the anxiety that had shadowed them the night before.

Perhaps he'd had a rough day at work, and she'd read too much into their dinner conversation or lack thereof.

Tom and Katy thanked her again and left.

When the tarts were done, Rachel removed them from the oven. "I need to run a couple of trays over to the neighbor's," she told Jimmy. "Do you want to come?"

"Do I have to?" he asked. "I'm doing a puzzle."

"No, you can stay. I'll be right back." She resisted the temptation to pilfer a couple of tarts before donning her oven mitts. Inhaling the delicious aroma as she walked to Tom's, she regretted her self-control.

Tom opened the kitchen door before she reached the stoop. He'd already changed into his uniform. His hair was damp from a shower, and a fresh, distinctly masculine scent floated about him. Reaching for one of the trays, he thanked her profusely.

"Don't touch!" Rachel squealed before he could touch the tray. "They're still hot."

"Thanks for the warning." He drew his hand back, then held the door open for her.

She entered the kitchen and glanced around the room. The table and all the countertops were filled with baked goodies as well as bowls and pans waiting to be washed. "You have been busy. Everything looks and smells amazing."

Tom cleared a spot on the counter for the trays she carried. He filled an empty foil pie pan with samples and handed it to her. "For you and Jimmy."

"I couldn't take any of your treats," Rachel said. "You need them for tomorrow's event."

"As you can see, we have plenty," he said, motioning to the baked goods on the table and counters. "I insist."

Rachel accepted the plate, thanked him, and headed home. As she got closer to the cottage, she thought she heard Jimmy crying, so she quickened her pace. The kitchen door was locked, and his crying grew louder.

"Jimmy, it's Mommy." She banged on the door and peeked through the window. "I'm right here. Unlock the door."

Jimmy's cries turned into an ear-piercing scream.

4

Panicked, Rachel dropped the plate of baked goods, gripped the doorknob, and jiggled it. She needed to get to her son. "Jimmy, Mommy's here. Let me in." Why hadn't she grabbed her key? She raced around to the front door, but it was locked too.

Jimmy's continued cries broke her heart.

She knocked loudly. "Jimmy, please let me in."

"No!"

Rachel plunged into the rosebushes guarding the front window and peered through the glass.

Jimmy stood by the bottom of the stairs, staring in the opposite direction, seemingly deaf to her voice and knocking. He shook his head and screamed, "No, you're lying!"

Someone's in there! Her heart pounding, she sprinted around to the mudroom. She snatched a log from the nearby woodpile and used it to smash the window. She quickly scraped the log around the window frame to clear away the shards, then hoisted herself through. "Jimmy, it's all right. Mommy's here." Brandishing the log, she dashed to the front of the house, ready to confront their intruder.

But there was no one in the room.

Jimmy threw himself at her legs, almost sending her toppling.

Regaining her balance, she dropped the log and folded him in her arms. "I've got you. You're okay."

Jimmy sobbed against her shoulder.

Tom rushed in from the direction of the mudroom. "What's going on? Is Jimmy hurt?"

Rachel skimmed her hands over her son's limbs and examined him from top to toe. There was no sign of bruising or any other injury. "Physically, he seems fine. But someone was here." She tightened her hold on her son and forced her voice down a few decibels. "*Is* here. I didn't see him run out. When I arrived, Jimmy was yelling at him."

"Stay here." Tom pulled a gun from a holster at his ankle and did a sweep of the rooms on the main floor before charging upstairs.

What felt like an eternity later, he returned, his gun now hidden once more in its holster. "There's no one here now."

Sirens filled the air, and a moment later, two police cruisers careened into the driveway.

"I'll bet Katy called 911." Tom opened the front door and disappeared outside.

Rachel coaxed Jimmy over to the sofa and cuddled the sobbing boy on her lap. "I'm here now, honey. I won't let anything bad happen to you. I'm so sorry you were frightened."

Jimmy sniffed loudly and buried his face in her sweater.

Tom returned with the plate of pastries she'd abandoned on the porch and set it on the coffee table. "I asked the officers to survey the grounds for evidence of a prowler."

Rachel couldn't stop shaking. She rested her cheek on the top of her son's head and rocked him. "I shouldn't have left him home alone. No one ever broke into our house in Boston. The possibility never occurred to me." *Maybe Richard is right, and we don't belong here.*

Tom's expression was serious. "You locked the doors when you left the house?"

"No, I didn't have a key on me," she answered, "and I thought I'd be gone only a minute. The front door was locked, but I went out the back door."

Tom disappeared into the kitchen and returned a moment later. "The lock on the doorknob was engaged."

"So, the intruder had already run out before I got through the window," Rachel concluded.

"Could you have activated the lock yourself out of habit as you left?"

She gaped at him. "Do you think I'm imagining intruders now? Someone was here."

"You saw the intruder?" Tom asked.

"No, I saw Jimmy through the window," she said. "He was standing at the bottom of the stairs, shouting at someone."

Tom traced the line of sight from the window to the base of the stairs and walked over. "You saw him standing about here?"

"Yes." Rachel fought to control the exasperation creeping into her voice.

"Facing that way?" Tom pointed to the right of the stairs.

She nodded.

Tom dropped to his knees, presumably so his line of sight would be at what Jimmy's had been. A moment later, he went to the telephone table to the right of the stairs and tapped a button on the phone.

Rachel swallowed hard as understanding dawned. She cupped Jimmy's chin and lifted it so their gazes met. "Did the phone ring when Mommy was out?"

Tears pooled in his eyes as he nodded.

"And you answered it?" she continued.

"I didn't mean to," Jimmy whined, clearly fearing he was in trouble. "I pressed the big white button to shut it off, like you do."

Tom studied the phone. "He pressed the speaker button."

Rachel sighed. "I guess that explains why he appeared to be talking to someone out of view."

Tom dropped to one knee beside Jimmy and squeezed his shoulder. "Now this is important. Can you tell me exactly what the caller said?"

Jimmy sniffed. "He asked for Mommy."

"What did you say?" Tom asked softly.

"I didn't tell him she wasn't here," Jimmy replied. "Mommy told me I'm not supposed to do that."

Anger shot through Rachel. Her son had done the right thing, but a caller had still managed to terrorize him.

"I told him she couldn't come to the phone right now," Jimmy went on. He glanced at her. "Just like you taught me."

"Good job," Rachel said encouragingly.

"Did you recognize the caller's voice?" Tom asked.

Jimmy shook his head. "He sounded like a robot."

Rachel gave Tom a panicked look. "The person deliberately disguised his voice to frighten us?"

"Or a computerized telemarketer phoned," Tom responded. "The caller ID lists the number as private."

Rachel exhaled in relief. She hadn't thought of that. Some of the telemarketing calls had gotten so sophisticated these days that their responses mimicked a real conversation. She wouldn't be surprised if they could fool a six-year-old into thinking he was talking to a real person on the other end. A real person who apparently sounded like a robot. She frowned. That didn't make sense. The robocalls always sounded like human beings.

"What did the caller say next?" Tom prompted.

Jimmy trembled.

Rachel tightened her hold. "It's okay. You're not in any trouble."

"He said bad things happen to liars," Jimmy replied, still trembling.

"You didn't lie," Rachel reassured Jimmy. "I couldn't come to the phone, and that's what you told him."

Jimmy dried his cheeks with the back of his sleeve. "Then he said even worse things happen to mothers who leave their son home alone." He gulped. "That's when I yelled, 'You're lying!'"

Rachel hugged Jimmy tight, her gaze locking with Tom's, silently pleading. "How did the caller know I left him alone?" she whispered.

Tom jumped to his feet. "I'll be right back."

"It turns out we're dealing with a crank caller, possibly of the stalker variety," Tom announced to the three officers who'd been searching the perimeter of the house for evidence of an intruder. "The caller seemed to know that Mrs. Sound had left the house, so he was probably lurking nearby. He could have parked on her street or walked or cycled by. It's possible that he was hiding out in one of the vacant summer homes. See if you can find him or anyone in the vicinity who can identify him."

"Seriously?" the rookie of the group scoffed. "What are the chances of catching a crank caller? We'd have better luck driving into town and nabbing jaywalkers."

Tom scowled at him. Though Jimmy may not have been in any real danger, they couldn't ignore the pranks any longer. "We're talking about a guy who's terrorizing a single mother and her son. And this may not be the first time."

"What else has happened?" the rookie asked.

Tom filled them in on the other events that had occurred at the cottage so far. "She's new to the island. This is not the kind of welcome we want her to receive."

The rookie's partner elbowed the newbie. "And she's Tom's neighbor. We protect our own."

"If another urgent call comes in, you're obviously free to answer it," Tom said. "But in the meantime, hunt down whatever clues you can find."

The three saluted and fanned out once more.

"Until we catch this guy," Tom called after them, "I'd appreciate it if you could do regular patrols this way to check for anyone who appears to be watching the house."

His own front screen door slammed shut, and Katy took a tentative step across the porch. She glanced at the officers, then dashed toward Tom. "Is Miss Sound okay?"

Tom gave his sister a hug. "She's a little shaken up, but she's fine. Good work calling 911."

Katy beamed.

"How about you go back to the house and find Jimmy the biggest gingerbread cookie we made and bring it over for me?" he suggested.

Katy squealed her approval and dashed off.

Tom returned to Rachel's living room. As much as he wanted to grill her about who might terrorize Jimmy, now wasn't the time. She'd clearly drawn on every ounce of her fortitude to hold herself together and comfort her rattled son.

"I asked the other officers to check the vicinity for anyone who noticed someone watching the house," he told her. "But the caller could have guessed you were out of the house based on the fact you weren't available to answer the phone."

Rachel nodded. "That makes me feel slightly better, but I can't believe anyone would be so cruel to a little boy."

"Sadly, we see all types, even on Martha's Vineyard."

A faint knock sounded at the door.

"Come in," she called.

Katy entered. Her bright smile chased the last shadows from Jimmy's countenance. "I brought you a treat." She handed the boy a plastic bag containing a giant gingerbread man. The icing belt and suspenders were dotted with jelly beans.

Jimmy widened his eyes. "For me?"

"You bet," Tom answered. "But your mom might want you to wait until after dinner to eat it. We don't want to spoil your supper."

"That's a good idea," Rachel agreed.

Sighing, Jimmy slipped off Rachel's lap and set his gingerbread man on the coffee table next to the plate of goodies.

"I suppose you'll be leaving for work soon?" Rachel asked Tom.

"Yes, I need to pack up the cookies and pastries and drive my sister home. But I'll do regular patrols past your place, and I've asked the other officers to as well."

Rachel ducked her head. "Thanks."

"I want you to feel safe here." Tom hated to leave them on such a somber note, so he asked Jimmy, "How would you and your mom like to come to Grandparents' Day with us tomorrow afternoon?"

Rachel flinched.

Tom wanted to kick himself for mentioning grandparents when Jimmy had recently lost his. "No grandparents required," he backpedaled. "It's more of a fun day for kids with games and a jumping house and lots of good food."

Jimmy bounced onto the sofa. "Can we, Mom? Please."

Rachel hesitated, biting her lip.

Tom gently added, "The older folks in the congregation don't all have grandkids on the island, and they love to do crafts with the kids too. My mom usually attends, but she won't be able to make it. I'm taking Katy with me."

"Can I think about it?" Rachel asked.

"Of course," Tom said. A breeze swept through the house, reminding him that she still had a broken window to address. "I'll board up that window for you before I head out."

"You don't have to do that," she protested. "I'm sure I can find a piece of plywood in the shed."

"It's no problem," Tom assured her. "I have half a sheet in the garage that will take care of it until you can get a repairman over."

"Thank you," Rachel said, her voice trembling. "I don't know what I would have done if you hadn't been here."

"You would have been fine. Your instincts are good." Tom squeezed her shoulder and was surprised by the jolt of awareness that tingled through his fingers. "Don't hesitate to call if you have any more trouble."

"I will," Rachel promised. Her cheeks grew pink. "Call, I mean."

He ignored the odd thump in his chest.

Twenty minutes later, Tom had the plywood cut to size and returned to Rachel's to mount it in place. Katy pitched in where she could.

Rachel came outside with Jimmy, a soccer ball tucked under her arm. "I really appreciate this."

"It's no trouble." Once Tom had the first couple of screws in place to hold the board, he released Katy to join the soccer game. He couldn't recall his mother ever kicking a ball around with him. Perhaps because that had been Dad's domain. Rachel was a great mom. She taught Jimmy how to kick the ball with the inside of his foot and shouted encouragements when the ball flew wildly in the opposite direction Jimmy had intended. Her hair shimmered in the sunshine, and her smile . . .

Tom shook his head and returned his attention to his work. He shouldn't be noticing Rachel's hair, let alone her smile. She was a victim of crimes. He was the investigating officer. There were boundaries to uphold.

Still, he lingered over the task longer than necessary.

5

Butterflies fluttered in her stomach as Rachel drove into the parking lot of Tom's church. The expansive lawn was filled with smiling people. There were tables of food and crafts and various game booths. A giant bouncy house filled the baseball diamond's infield, and a rowdy game of touch football took place in the outfield.

"Billy's over there." Jimmy pointed to his friend standing in line at the bouncy house. "Can I go?"

Rachel parked. "Yes. I'll catch up with you when you're done."

Jimmy jumped out of his booster seat and opened his car door.

"Watch for cars," Rachel warned as her son bolted toward his friend.

Rachel spotted Tom playing football and wandered over to watch. Teens and college kids played against their dads and other men. She recognized several students from school. Ian, the teen whose father had pressed her to waive his academic probation, was a different person on the field. Confident and focused, he seemed alert to everyone's position and intention. If only there were a way to funnel his passion for the game into his studies.

Tom hurled a long pass to one of his teammates, but Ian intercepted it. The instant his feet hit the ground, he dashed for the opposite goal line.

Rachel clapped and cheered.

Jogging past her, Tom mock scowled. "You're supposed to be cheering for my side."

She laughed. "But he's my student."

Blake sidled up to her. "Ian's good, isn't he?"

Bracing herself for a repeat episode of school's opening day pleas, she agreed his son had talent.

"I didn't realize you were James Sound's widow," Blake remarked. "I used to spend every summer with him and his brother. The three of us were inseparable. We'd go swimming, sailing, and fishing."

"You did?" At the last second, Rachel managed to temper the longing that had crept into her voice. She'd love to hear more about her husband's summers on the island, but she had the uneasy sense Blake had merely mentioned the relationship to win her over.

Seemingly changing tack, Blake motioned toward the craft tables. "Is that your son?"

Rachel glanced over. "Yes, that's him." Jimmy and his friend were no longer at the bouncy house. Now they were enthusiastically painting popsicle sticks with a couple of grinning seniors.

"How old is he?"

"Six," she replied. After what happened to Jimmy the day before, Blake's questions about her son made her skin crawl. She wished she'd stayed at Jimmy's side where she belonged. "Excuse me, please. I should join him."

Blake shifted, effectively blocking her escape. "As a parent, I'm sure you'd do whatever it takes to ensure your son succeeds."

Rachel gritted her teeth. The man's implication was clear. The question was: What did he think it would take for *his* son to succeed? Scaring her into leaving her teaching position? Intimidating her until she bent to his will?

Tom jogged over to them and placed a warm hand on her shoulder. "Glad you made it."

Blake immediately excused himself. "It was nice talking to you. Maybe I can dig out some old photos of James for you next time."

"That would be nice. Thank you." Rachel forced a smile. "We could discuss possible options for Ian too."

"Count on it," Blake said, his tone harsh. He stalked away.

"Are you all right?" Tom asked as soon as Blake was out of earshot.

Rachel's heart warmed at the realization that Tom had noticed Blake getting to her. She nodded. "I am now."

"I'm concerned that Blake sees you as the main roadblock to his son playing football."

"His probation wasn't my call," Rachel said. "He knows that."

"Sure, but that might be the only thing Blake cares about now."

She scanned the field and followed Ian's playing for a few moments. "I would be thrilled if Ian was able to play. He's obviously gifted at sports. And I know from experience that denying kids the opportunity to do what they love won't help them apply themselves to their academics—not if they can't see any hope of the extra effort making a difference."

"You don't think he's capable of getting a C?"

"I haven't seen any evidence in the classroom of him making the effort," Rachel admitted. "But watching him play today, he seems like a different kid. If I could figure out where the gaps are in his academics and somehow channel his confidence and ambition from the field into his studies, I'm sure he'd show a marked improvement in his grades."

Tom grinned. "I wish I'd had a teacher like you in high school."

Her face heated. She ducked her head so Tom wouldn't see her blush. "I should check on Jimmy."

He fell into step beside her. "I'm sorry Blake bothered you. I was hoping today's events would be a welcome escape from the stresses in your life."

Rachel chewed on her bottom lip. "Have you had any leads on who called the house yesterday?"

"No, I'm sorry."

"It's creepy to imagine someone watching our place." She cringed and glanced around. "Maybe someone is watching us right now."

"I doubt it," Tom said.

"I know you think the caller made a good guess based on Jimmy's response," she commented.

He didn't respond, but a muscle twitched in his cheek.

Rachel narrowed her eyes. She got the distinct sense he was holding something back. "What is it?"

"Another option occurred to me while I was on patrol last night," Tom said. "If the caller is the same person who hacked into your smart system, that could be how he knew you left the house."

Her heart pinched. "How? We don't have any security cameras hooked to the system."

"No, but he could listen in on conversations through the computer," he said. "Or maybe he even watched the room through the computer's camera."

At Rachel's startled reaction, Tom regretted voicing his concern.

Rachel pushed a hand through her hair, then made a beeline for Jimmy at the crafts table.

Tom trailed after her. "I'm sorry. Causing you more worry was the last thing I wanted to do."

"Don't be." She stopped just shy of the table where her son was assembling a popsicle-stick house. "I need to know these things if I'm going to protect Jimmy. But I don't think I had the computer on."

"That's good," he responded. "Then the fact that you weren't home was probably a lucky guess on the caller's part. Have you thought of anyone who'd want to harass you?"

Seeming a fraction less worried now that her son was nearby, Rachel sighed. "You mean besides Blake?"

Tom studied the man still watching the football game. "I'll check into his whereabouts. Is there anyone else? Perhaps an ex-boyfriend?"

"I haven't dated anyone since my husband died three years ago."

He tried to ignore his mixed feelings at that revelation. "I have to admit I'm suspicious of Ellen Donovan."

"The substitute teacher at school?" she asked.

"Yes, she'd hoped to be chosen for the position they hired you for."

"I had no idea. Ellen must hate me. Who could blame her for lashing out? She's worked at the school for a while." Rachel frowned. "But I can't believe any teacher could frighten a child over the phone that way."

"You might be right," Tom said. "I could see Ellen pulling up stakes in the school garden and hiding the bulletin board, but I'm not sure she's tech savvy enough to hack into your smart system."

She lowered her gaze.

"What is it?" he asked. "Did you think of someone else?"

Rachel winced. "I didn't want to mention him before."

"Who?"

"My brother-in-law." She lowered her voice. "Richard was angry when his parents left me their cottage. The will stipulates that if I don't live there full-time for the first two years, ownership reverts to the estate. So Richard has a good reason to make my life miserable by sabotaging my teaching career or otherwise scaring me out of the cottage."

"Do you really think he would terrify his own nephew?" Tom asked. The very idea made him feel ill.

Rachel didn't answer, but the wariness in her eyes was unmistakable.

"Has he verbally threatened you?"

She shook her head. "He's a lawyer in Boston, so he knows better. He contested the will, though. But I recently learned the judge ruled against him, so that might have prompted him to resort to other tactics."

"I doubt a Boston attorney would have made a trip to Martha's Vineyard to trash your school garden or hide your bulletin board," he said. "But if those were student pranks or Ellen's handiwork, it would explain the difference in the level of malice behind the hacking and phone call."

"Except I don't think Richard would need to hack into the smart system," Rachel told him. "I'm sure he knows the password and maybe even has the app on his phone from his many visits to his parents' cottage. And your tech guy didn't find evidence of anyone logging in, right? Wasn't that how you knew it wasn't Jimmy?"

"Not exactly," Tom answered. "Your system was toggled to the option of remaining logged in. Jimmy wouldn't need to know the password. But there was no activity on the app on your computer that night. The instructions originated from somewhere else, but there was no record of the person's IP address."

"So, our hacker was knowledgeable enough to know how to cover his electronic tracks?"

"Apparently."

"I doubt Richard could manage that," she said. "Please forget I mentioned him. He might be the only one who's exhibited any animosity of late, but it is uncharacteristic of him. I think he took his parents' sudden deaths really hard."

"I can understand that," he said. "If you think of anyone else, let me know."

Rachel agreed, then listened as Jimmy gave her a tour of his popsicle-stick house.

Tom watched her interact with her son. Jimmy seemed like a terrific kid. "Great job on your house. How about an ice cream cone?"

"Yes!" Jimmy whooped. "Can we, Mom?"

She smiled. "Sure."

Katy, who'd been helping at the face-painting booth, joined them for ice cream, and Rachel seemed to relax.

After they finished their cones, Katy convinced Jimmy to be her partner in a three-legged race. Rachel was soon in stitches from their comical hand-waving, hip-swaying movements. Tom didn't know which he enjoyed more—watching the kids or Rachel.

Tom had naturally felt concern for victims of crime before, but it had never haunted him like the concern he felt for Rachel. Yes, he was attracted to her, but he couldn't take advantage of her vulnerability. She hadn't dated since her husband's death. Maybe she wasn't ready. Maybe she'd never be ready.

The event ended at four, but Tom had volunteered to help clean up afterward, so he and Katy said their goodbyes to Rachel and Jimmy.

By the time he drove his sister home, dusk had settled in. The leaves hadn't dropped from the trees yet, but he could still see the dappled lights of Rachel's place through them as he drove up their road. He did a double take. Were those parking lights?

Suddenly, the vehicle careened onto the road and headed toward him.

Tom braked, hoping to catch a glimpse of the driver.

The woman behind the wheel glanced his way, then sped off.

But Tom recognized her. It was Ellen Donovan.

6

Tom pulled into Rachel's driveway rather than following Ellen. He could find out where she lived easily enough. He'd noted the make and model of her vehicle, and he'd gotten her license plate number as she'd sped away.

Rachel appeared from behind the house, holding barbecue tongs and a plate with two grilled burgers on it. She smiled as she approached his truck. "You're just in time for dinner. Would you like a burger?"

"No thanks. I only wanted to check in," he said nonchalantly. "Did you see any sign anyone had nosed around the place while you were out?"

"No." She inhaled deeply as if bracing herself. "Nothing seems amiss. The street's been quiet. I heard a car slow, so that's why I came out. It must have been you."

Tom didn't bother telling her the car she'd heard was likely Ellen's. He'd decided to ask Ellen herself for an explanation. "That's good. I'll see you later." He backed out of the driveway, but instead of going home, he headed in the direction Ellen had been traveling and called his buddy who was working the afternoon shift. "Are you in your cruiser?"

"Yeah. Why?"

"Can you find an address for the driver of a blue Toyota Camry?" Tom recited the license plate number.

His friend chuckled. "The guy cut you off?"

"No, I spotted the car loitering outside my neighbor's place."

"The car belongs to Ellen Donovan." His buddy gave him the woman's address. "Want me to pay her a visit?"

"That's okay. I'll handle this. Thanks." Tom disconnected and headed for Ellen's house.

Ten minutes later, he parked behind Ellen's car in her driveway. He peeked inside her car as he headed toward the front porch, but there was nothing visible inside to corroborate his suspicions. No binoculars. No crowbar. No listening device.

Ellen answered his knock with a welcoming smile. "What a nice surprise."

"I was wondering if you have a minute," Tom said.

"Come in." She stepped back, opening the door wide, and motioned him inside. "Can I get you a cup of coffee?"

"No thanks," he said as he followed her into the living room.

Ellen sat down on the sofa. "I didn't realize you knew where I lived."

He took a seat in the armchair across from her. "I saw you near my place and looked you up in the system." Rather than mirroring her friendly tone, he kept his neutral.

Her smile suddenly seemed rigid.

Tom waited for her to fill in the ensuing silence with an explanation, as guilty parties usually did, and she didn't disappoint.

"You did?" Ellen squeaked. "My dad lives not far from you."

He didn't respond.

Once again, she filled the silence. "Yeah, he, um, invited me to pick some of his butternut squash if I wanted them. He had a bumper crop this year."

"He's fortunate," he said, attempting to bait her. "My mom lost her plants to squash vine borers this year."

"Let me give you a couple of them for her." Ellen hurried out of the room and returned with two large squashes, still bearing the odd remnant of dirt. She handed them over.

"Are you sure?" Given her generosity, Tom felt guilty for doubting her story.

"Absolutely. I have plenty for myself." She returned to her seat on the couch. "So, why did you drop in?"

"I was wondering if you happened to be out my way yesterday afternoon."

"Yesterday?" Ellen fiddled with the throw covering the back of the sofa. "No, I don't think so. I went to the flea market with friends."

"The flea market isn't open after Labor Day, is it?"

"You're right," she said. "I meant the farmers market. Why?"

"It's not important," he answered. "Not if you weren't that way."

"You're sure I can't interest you in a drink? Iced tea?"

"No thanks. I need to be going." Tom held up the squashes. "And thanks for these."

As he walked to his car, he considered the visit. Ellen had definitely been unnerved by his arrival. If she had been behind the incidents, now that she knew he'd seen her in the vicinity, hopefully she'd be afraid of being spotted again.

And with any luck that would keep her from causing Rachel any more trouble.

Monday after school, Rachel gave her son a puzzle to assemble at a table in the back of her classroom while she met with Ian and his father to discuss his academic probation. "Did you bring your notebooks?" she asked Ian.

The teen retrieved a stack of spiral-bound notebooks from his backpack. Each had his name neatly printed on the front and the name of a class.

As Rachel reached for the red notebook on the top of the stack, a loose page drifted to the floor.

Blake snatched it up.

She noticed how similar it was to the paper Tom had found near her destroyed garden the first day of school. But the handwriting wasn't Ian's. "What's that?" she asked.

"The exercise regimen Ian received over the summer to get ready for this season," Blake explained. He showed her the chart filled with check marks.

Rachel nodded. "I'm impressed by your dedication to your assigned exercises, Ian. If you're as conscientious about doing remedial studies, then perhaps we can make this football season work for you after all."

Ian's face lit up.

"I'm not making any promises," she warned. "You have to apply yourself and put in the work."

"He will," his father promised.

Ian, however, slouched in his chair, clearly betraying his own doubts.

"So, his coach wrote this program for him?" Rachel tapped the notepaper.

"No, Davis did," Blake replied.

She'd never even met Trent Davis. Why would the PE teacher pull any crazy pranks on her? Unless it was some kind of initiation for new teachers. Or . . . "Did he give every player a sheet like this?"

Blake turned to Ian for the answer, but his son only shrugged.

Rachel pushed the thought aside. She didn't even know if the paper Tom found belonged to her prankster. For all she knew, it had blown across the schoolyard from somewhere else.

Rachel returned the paper to Ian and read through his notes and assignments in the notebooks. Spelling was a challenge, but at least he'd attempted all his assignments, as scant as his answers were.

After her confrontation with Blake, she'd reviewed Ian's school records. His primary teachers had frequently called him bright, but they bemoaned his inattention. His later teachers merely said he needed to put in more effort. Ian had attended remedial classes in his early years, but there was no mention that he'd taken assessments for potential learning disabilities.

Rachel surveyed the contents of each notebook, then closed the last one and straightened the stack. "I'd like you to come in after school tomorrow to do a couple of assessments that will help me gauge where we should focus extra attention."

"But practices are after school," Ian reminded her.

"I haven't agreed to waive your probation yet," she said sternly. "I'm not giving you a free pass. You have to work for it. I'll talk with Mr. Sutton about options and see what I can do."

Frowning, Ian stuffed the notebooks back into his backpack.

"Chin up," Rachel said in a chipper voice. "You wouldn't approach a game with this kind of posture and attitude, would you?"

Ian straightened. "No ma'am."

"Good," she said. "I want you to bring your full attention to our remedial sessions. Okay?"

Ian nodded, then slid from his chair and shuffled toward the door.

"I trust you're not raising my boy's hopes for nothing," Blake said.

"I want to see Ian succeed," Rachel told him, "but he has to make the effort."

Blake rapped his knuckles on the student desk his son had occupied a moment earlier. "Fair enough. We'll see you tomorrow."

She hoped Blake didn't plan on sitting through their remedial sessions.

Rachel and Ian didn't need the pressure. She jotted down a couple of things she needed to remember to prepare for the next day's session.

She texted Tom. *I'm not sure if it means anything, but the paper you found by my trashed garden on opening day was written by the PE teacher, likely for one of his football players. Ian had a similar page in his notebook.*

Tom didn't reply.

"Can we go home now?" Jimmy asked.

"We're leaving soon," Rachel said, slipping her phone into her purse. "You can start putting the puzzle away. I need to run to the supply closet to collect supplies to take home to prep for my class tomorrow."

Suddenly, she worried about leaving her son alone, but she needed to get past this fear. She took a calming breath. She would be gone for only a few minutes, and he would be fine here in her classroom.

Aside from the odd straggler, the hall was devoid of students. The school buses had already collected their riders, so the only students remaining were those attending after-school clubs or waiting for rides. She switched on the light in the walk-in closet and made her way to the back where the colored poster board was stored.

The room went dark.

"I'm in here," she called out.

The door shut, and the lock clicked.

"Hey!" Rachel stumbled over a box in her rush to get to the door. Aside from a sliver of light seeping under the bottom of the door, the room was pitch-black. She limped the rest of the way to the door and tried the handle. The door didn't budge. She slapped the door with her open palm. "You locked me in. Let me out!"

Nothing happened.

She banged on the door and shouted louder, then pressed her ear to the door. Whoever had locked it couldn't have gotten far in such a short amount of time. Why wasn't he opening the door? Surely, he could hear her shouting.

Unless someone had locked her inside the supply closet deliberately.

Her stomach lurched. Jimmy was alone in her classroom. What if this creep tried to lure him away by lying about her leaving, as the caller had done?

Rachel pounded on the door. "Help! I'm locked in the closet. Please let me out." She reached into her pocket for her cell phone, but it wasn't there. She'd slipped it into her purse after texting Tom.

Her heart raced. *Please, Lord, let Jimmy be okay. Bring someone to find me.* She felt around the doorknob for the lock release, something that hadn't occurred to her in her panic, but the knob was smooth. She banged on the door again and yelled for help.

Her voice grew hoarse, and her hand burned. Then she heard voices. "I'm in here!" she shouted. "Please let me out."

She rejoiced at the scrape of the key in the dead bolt.

A moment later, the door opened.

Rachel squinted at the sudden bright light. She saw Katy and Jack, the custodian, in the doorway.

"How did you lock yourself in there?" Katy asked.

"I didn't," Rachel said. "Someone locked me in."

"Who was it?" Jack asked.

Rachel shrugged. "I don't know."

"Well, you have Katy to thank for not having to spend the night in there," Jack said jovially. "The school's almost empty."

"Jimmy!" Rachel pushed past them and dashed down the hall toward her classroom. She skidded to a stop at the door. "I'm sorry I took so long—" She froze.

The classroom was empty.

7

Rachel raced up the school's hallway, calling her son's name as she poked her head into each classroom. Reaching the main doors, she shoved them open. Jimmy wasn't in the parking lot. "Jimmy, where are you?"

"I found him!" Katy shouted.

Rachel hurried down the side hallway that hosted the elementary school classrooms. Her heart squeezed at the sight of Jimmy standing beside Katy in the middle of the hall.

"He was in the bathroom," Katy explained.

Rachel rushed over and swept her son into a hug. "I was so worried when I couldn't find you."

"I tried waiting for you, but I couldn't hold it any longer," Jimmy said defensively.

Rachel laughed. "It's not your fault."

"Your mom got locked in the closet," Katy interjected.

Rachel winced. She didn't want to worry Jimmy. "I'm ready to go now," she said in the cheeriest voice she could muster. Her quest for supplies could wait until morning.

Jack came around the corner. "Your mom's here to pick you up," he said to Katy.

Rachel frowned. She was disappointed that Tom wasn't coming to get his sister as he'd done last week. She wanted to believe that getting locked in the supply closet was an accident, but what if it wasn't? She would have liked Tom's perspective on the situation.

"Bye." Katy waved at Jimmy enthusiastically.

Jimmy mirrored her enthusiasm.

"Thanks for helping me," Rachel called after the bubbly teen. "You were a godsend."

Smiling, Katy dashed off.

Rachel thanked Jack for rescuing her from the supply closet too, then collected her purse and jacket from the classroom and headed out to her car with Jimmy.

Before they were a mile down the road, her cell phone rang. She tapped the phone button on the dashboard to answer. "Hello?"

It was her lawyer. "I'm afraid I have bad news," Lauren said.

"What is it?" Rachel asked, bracing herself for the worst.

"Your brother-in-law filed an appeal of the judge's ruling about your in-laws' will today," Lauren replied. "I'm sorry."

Rachel's shoulders sank. At the mere thought of being dragged into court again, exhaustion swept over her. "I'm afraid I'll have to defend myself this time." *Before Richard bleeds me dry in lawyer's fees.* He was an attorney, so legal fees were an expense he didn't have. No doubt he was using that to his advantage.

"I understand," Lauren said. "Call me if you change your mind."

Tapping the receiver off, Rachel huffed out a sigh, then glanced in the rearview mirror at Jimmy. He was quieter than normal. "What did you do in school today?"

Instead of answering the question, he asked, "Why is Uncle Richard mad at us?"

She regretted taking the call with Jimmy in the car. "He's not mad. He's sad over losing his parents, your grandma and grandpa." She wanted to say he was lashing out, but that sounded like he was mad. How could she phrase his actions in a way Jimmy wouldn't take personally? "Your uncle is struggling to accept the loss and the way things have changed because of it."

"He never comes to see us anymore."

"Coming to visit isn't as easy for him now that we live here," Rachel explained. "When we lived with your grandparents in Boston, he could easily stop by after work or on the weekends and see us all at the same time."

Jimmy expelled a huff of air. "I guess." He stared out the window at the moving scenery. "Can we see Tom tonight?"

Her heart skipped a beat. She needed to talk to Tom about the supply closet incident, so she wouldn't mind seeing him either, but was Jimmy getting too attached to their helpful neighbor? Was she?

Rachel tightened her grip on the steering wheel. Letting herself care about Tom was a bad idea. Everyone she ever cared about had been taken away—her parents, James, and now his parents.

Catching sight of Jimmy in the rearview mirror again, she was overwhelmed with love for him. She couldn't bear for anything to happen to her sweet son too. Rachel pasted on a smile. "How would you like to pick up pizza and have a picnic on the beach?"

"Yeah!" Jimmy shouted.

His resounding approval bolstered her own sagging energy, and she grinned. "We can watch the fishermen surf casting."

The island's annual fishing derby had begun the day before. Although Rachel had never been here during the derby, she'd heard a lot about it. Everyone seemed eager to get in as much fishing time as they could, which was probably why the school had cleared out so quickly after the last bell. With any luck, they'd see some interesting fish hauled in.

Best of all, the fresh air would wear them out for an early night's sleep. She planned to go to school early tomorrow so she could do the prep work she'd planned to do tonight.

At the thought of returning to school, Rachel felt a sense of dread. What was going to happen next?

Tom shifted the paperwork on his desk in search of his beeping phone. It was a text message from Katy. *I rescued Miss Sound from the supply closet at school.*

His pulse quickened, and he phoned his sister. "What happened?"

"Someone locked the teacher in the closet after school, and she couldn't get out," Katy answered. "No one was around to hear her shouting. But Mom was late to pick me up, so I was walking around and heard her and got Mr. Drew, the custodian, so he could let her out."

"You did the right thing," Tom said. "Did she see who shut the door?"

"No, and then she got scared because she couldn't find Jimmy," she said. "He was in the bathroom. I found him too."

He grimaced as he imagined how frantic Rachel had been when she couldn't locate her son. "Good work. I'm proud of you. I'm sure she was grateful you were there."

"She called me a godsend," Katy said.

Tom smiled at the awe in his sister's voice. "That you are. I've got to get back to work, but thanks for letting me know. I'll see you soon." He clicked off.

Was Rachel's prankster back to his or her old tricks? He wondered if Ellen had been at school today. He'd hoped he'd sufficiently spooked her out of pulling any more stunts—if she was the one behind them.

Tom checked his phone to make sure he hadn't missed a call from Rachel. Would she call to update him on this latest incident? Or would she write it off as unrelated? She might be embarrassed to learn Katy had told him, but then again, Rachel had to assume that would happen.

Tom stacked his paperwork on his desk. His shift had already ended, and there was nothing in the pile that couldn't wait.

He swung by the post office and collected his mail. He was pleasantly surprised to recognize Rachel's car outside the pizza place next door. When she and her son emerged from the shop, he sauntered over to meet them. "Howdy, neighbor. How's your day?" he asked with a cowboy drawl that won him a giggle from Jimmy.

Rachel smiled. "It's great. Jimmy and I are going to have a pizza picnic on the beach to watch the fishermen. Would you like to come with us?"

"Yes, I'd love to." Encouraged to see that her supply closet ordeal hadn't cast a shadow over her day, Tom decided not to bring it up. Katy could be prone to exaggeration, or she might have misunderstood the situation.

"You're not signed up for the derby?" Rachel asked. "It seems like everyone is."

Tom laughed. "Oh, I'm signed up. I participate every year."

"Can I fish?" Jimmy tugged on Rachel's jacket sleeve. "Please."

"How about I stop at home to get my fishing gear?" Tom suggested. "I have a fishing rod that's the perfect size for Jimmy. Then I'll meet you at your house so we can ride together."

Rachel regarded him as if he'd hung the moon. "You wouldn't mind?"

"Of course not. I love to encourage junior fishermen." Grinning, Tom added, "I have a rod you can use too."

She held up her hands and took a step back. "Oh no. That's okay. I'm happy to simply watch."

"You're sure?"

"Positive," Rachel said. "You go on and get your gear. As soon as the pizza's ready, we'll head home."

Tom saluted. Feeling a whole lot lighter than he had when he left the station, he jumped into his truck and headed home. Rachel's smile had a way of lifting his mood like nothing he'd ever experienced.

Even Sarah, the woman he'd dated seriously for more than a year, hadn't seemed to brighten a room when she entered it. Then again, she'd been obsessed with having a houseful of kids, and the idea had petrified him.

Not that Tom didn't love kids. He did. He absolutely adored his kid sister. But he also remembered how much his parents had struggled to help Katy through her health issues. The long hospital stays in Boston. How his dad had worked himself into an early grave to pay the bills, leaving Mom even more bereft of support. Tom didn't want to do that to anyone.

With a heavy sigh, he shoved aside that thought. Going on a picnic with Rachel and her son wasn't exactly a date. By her own admission, she hadn't dated since her husband's death. She probably wasn't ready for it. Even if she were, she might not be interested in remarrying and having more children.

Tom shook the wayward notion from his head. This was crazy. He was joining a family for supper and fishing—that was all. Rachel probably only invited him because she was still nervous about the pranks and figured she'd be safer with a cop along.

He sighed in relief. That made sense. But cops still shouldn't be noticing the heartwarming smiles of victims of crimes they were investigating.

As he drove past Rachel's property, he caught sight of a dark vehicle parked beside her house. He threw his pickup into reverse and parked at the end of the driveway to block the prowler's escape. Glad he was still in his police uniform, he exited the truck and crept up the driveway, using the cover of the trees lining it.

No one was visible in the vehicle or at the front of the house. But as Tom circled toward the rear, a man came around the corner. Thanks to his training, Tom was able to analyze him in an instant. He was six foot two, hefty build, dark hair, narrow face, clean-shaven, black coat, black pants, black shoes. Then Tom squinted at the man's coat. There appeared to be something in his pocket—a gun?

Tom's cell phone chimed a text message alert.

At the sound, the man whirled toward the trees and plunged his hand into his coat pocket.

Tom drew his weapon and stepped into view. "Police. Freeze."

8

At the sight of Tom's truck parked across the end of her driveway, Rachel felt her pulse quicken. Had he caught an intruder? She didn't dare trudge up the driveway with Jimmy and risk exposing him to danger.

But would calling Tom's cell phone endanger him? What if he hadn't revealed himself to the prowler yet? Or he could be hurt, taken by surprise by the intruder.

She slowed her vehicle and peered through the trees. A black Range Rover was parked by the house. It was the same vehicle her brother-in-law drove. With anger overpowering fear, she slammed on her brakes and parked alongside the road.

"Why did Tom block our driveway?" Jimmy asked.

Rachel stepped out of the car. "I suspect he spotted Uncle Richard's SUV and thought we might have a prowler."

"Uncle Richard's here?" Jimmy scrambled out of his booster seat and sprang out the other side of the car.

"Hang on." Rachel caught his hand. "I'm not positive it's your uncle." They strode up the driveway, and she grimaced at the *Rainmaker* vanity plate.

"Uncle Richard!" Jimmy shouted, catching sight of his uncle accompanied by Tom.

Richard stood an inch or two shorter than Tom, his salt-and-pepper hair neatly trimmed. Richard's hands were behind his back.

Seeing Jimmy running toward them, Tom stepped behind Richard.

An instant later, Richard scooped up Jimmy and swung him high in the air as his father once had. Tom slid what Rachel guessed to be a set of handcuffs into his pocket.

Rachel hid a smile. She wished she'd seen Tom slap cuffs on Richard. But she hoped Richard didn't end up suing him for excessive force or wrongful arrest or something. She'd have to impress on her brother-in-law that Tom had been concerned for her welfare—well, Jimmy's if she wanted the argument to carry any weight.

Tom searched her eyes.

"Thanks for being here," Rachel whispered, then addressed Richard. "This is a surprise. What brings you over?" she asked as sweetly as she could manage.

Richard propped Jimmy on one arm and pretended to steal his nose. "I came to see my favorite nephew."

Richard resembled James so much that her heart ached at the sight of Jimmy looking so happy to be held in his arms. She couldn't believe Richard had the nerve to come here and play the doting uncle after the torment he'd put her through since his parents' deaths. Not to mention his filing another appeal just today.

"Richard heard you had a break-in," Tom interjected, probably sensing the head of steam she'd been building. "Apparently, his old friend Blake Culp listens to a police scanner and recognized the address of his parents' cottage when my sister called the station Saturday afternoon."

Rachel cocked her head. "Strange that Blake didn't mention it to us Sunday when I talked to him. Or during our meeting this afternoon."

"Isn't it?" Tom asked. "I explained to Richard what really happened."

"Blake didn't realize you were living here." Richard jostled Jimmy. "You were a brave boy to give that nasty caller what for." He sounded proud of his nephew. "You know your mommy would never let anything bad happen to you."

Rachel couldn't stop herself from gaping at his uncharacteristic vote of confidence. Then her head cleared, and she decided Richard was merely trying a different approach to get what he wanted.

"I'll arrange for the window to be replaced," Richard offered.

"That isn't necessary," she said. "I've already ordered a replacement and scheduled the installation."

"Send me the bill," Richard said, "and I'll take care of it."

Rachel shook her head. "I appreciate the offer, but it's my responsibility."

"We're going on a picnic," Jimmy blurted out. He grinned at Richard. "You want to come with us?"

Richard glanced at her as if seeking permission.

Her skin crawled. But Jimmy bounced in his arms so eagerly. How could Rachel deny him time with his one and only uncle? Against her common sense and every instinct in her body, she said, "Of course you're welcome to come if you have time."

"Great," Richard said. "I have my fishing gear along too. I was hoping to get some derby fishing in while on the island."

Rachel tensed. How long did he plan to stay? And where did he plan to sleep?

"I rented the cottage around the corner for the week, the one with the yard that backs onto yours," Richard said as if reading her mind. Sporting a wide grin, he patted Jimmy's chest. "Family or not, I thought it might be uncomfortable for you to have another man under the roof."

It was the understatement of the year, considering that the last time she'd seen him he swore the cottage would never be hers.

Sensing Tom edging away and likely about to bow out of joining them, Rachel caught his arm. "Tom's coming with us too," she informed Richard.

"No, that's okay," Tom said. "I don't want to intrude on your family time."

"You won't be," she insisted. Holding his gaze, she silently pleaded with him to agree.

Tom smiled. "Give me a few minutes to change and get that fishing gear like I promised. I'll meet you there." He strode to his truck.

"I'll drive separately if you don't mind," Richard said. "The best bass fishing is after sunset. I imagine that Jimmy will need to go to bed before I'm ready to call it quits."

"Yes, thank you," Rachel said. She didn't know what to make of this new version of Richard.

But no matter what he said, she still didn't trust him.

When Tom arrived at home, he changed his clothes, then grabbed a tin of gingerbread cookies left over from the Grandparents' Day celebration to contribute to their picnic.

Rachel pulled into his driveway as he was locking the house. "Ride with us?" she called out her window.

He couldn't help but notice the passenger seat. Empty.

"Richard is driving himself," she said. "He plans to stay late to keep fishing. Do you want to stay late too?"

"No, I have an early court appearance tomorrow morning." Tom handed her the tin of cookies through her open window. "My fishing gear is in the truck." A few moments later, he returned with his rods and tackle.

Rachel got out and opened the trunk. "Thank you so much for joining us."

He loaded the gear into her car. "It didn't seem like you wanted to be alone with Richard."

"You've got that right." Her eyes twinkled. "How did he react to your putting him in cuffs?"

"Not well," Tom answered. "But given his excuse for scoping out the back of the house when you weren't home, he couldn't protest too much."

"When are we going?" Jimmy called from the back seat.

Rachel closed the trunk. "Right now."

Tom would have to question Rachel about her brother-in-law later. The aroma of pizza welcomed him into the vehicle. He inhaled deeply. "It smells good."

"We got two pizzas," Jimmy said. "And extra meat."

"That's the way I like it." Tom lifted the two large boxes from the passenger seat and held them on his lap. It was a good thing they had plenty of food now that her brother-in-law had crashed the party.

Richard waited for them in his idling SUV at the end of the driveway and trailed them down the road.

Tom studied the reflection of the man's vehicle in the side mirror. "Is Richard a good lawyer or just full of himself?"

Rachel smiled. "You mean his vanity license plate?"

Tom nodded.

"A little of both," she said. "He's the youngest partner at the firm, so he must be good. The vanity plate was a gift from my husband when Richard made partner."

"Was your husband a lawyer too?"

"No. He hated sitting behind a desk. He was an electrician."

"Residential?"

"For the most part," Rachel answered. "He liked to joke about his rates. His hourly rate was pretty standard, but he said if you wanted to watch, it would be thirty bucks more an hour. If you wanted to help, he'd add fifty. And if he was fixing your mistake, he'd add a hundred."

Tom chuckled. "I had an uncle who was a doctor by profession, but he did his own home maintenance. He lived by the motto waste not, want not."

"Oh no."

"You can see where this is going. Most of the time, my aunt called a professional the next day to fix what my uncle had done wrong."

Rachel laughed. She seemed relaxed.

Tom was glad he'd agreed to come.

They parked right on the beach, and Richard pulled up beside them. The men unloaded their fishing gear, and Rachel removed the food and drinks and a blanket from her car. The air was still, and the shore was dotted with fishermen.

Rachel smoothed out her blanket on the sand. "I've never seen so many people fishing here at one time."

"It's because of the derby." Richard spread out a blanket he'd brought along.

Jimmy plopped down on his uncle's blanket, leaving Tom to share the blanket with Rachel.

The conversation over supper remained light. They talked about fishing, which led to tales of Richard and his twin brother's summer childhood adventures on the island. Tom sensed Richard might be trying to bait Rachel into a reaction with some of his questions about school or the cottage, but she deftly changed the subject. However, once the pizza boxes and tin of cookies were bare and the soda bottles drained, the conversation grew stilted.

"I think it's time to fish," Tom declared. He smiled at Jimmy. "Would you like me to get you started?"

Jimmy sprang to his feet with a delighted squeal that could rival Katy's. Rachel threw away the boxes and paper plates while Tom instructed Jimmy in the art of surf casting.

Apparently fearing for his safety, Richard shifted a good distance down the shore to do his own fishing.

That suited Tom. Jimmy loved the activity, and Tom was more than happy to spend the evening supervising him rather than fishing himself.

Jimmy's line dipped deeper into the water. "I got something!" He jumped up and down and almost lost his rod in his excitement.

Tom caught it. He stood behind the boy and helped him hold the rod steady and reel in his catch. The bass splashed in the shallow water. With one final haul, Jimmy caught his first fish.

"It's a beauty," Tom said, ruffling Jimmy's hair. He searched the beach for Rachel. His pulse quickened when he didn't see her. Where was she?

He glanced around. Richard was a stone's throw away, completely focused on his line in the water, but there was no sign of Rachel.

"Come on," Tom said to Jimmy, trying to keep his concern from sounding in his voice. "Let's find your mom and show her your catch."

"Searching for me?" Rachel called out.

Tom released his pent-up breath. "Yes. Jimmy has something to show you."

She jogged over to them. "Sorry. I was in the restroom."

Jimmy beamed and held up his fish. "See what I caught?"

Rachel admired his catch. "That's a big one. We can eat it for tomorrow's supper."

"I can fillet it for you," Tom volunteered.

"Thanks," she said. "I'd appreciate it."

"Can I show Uncle Richard?" Jimmy asked eagerly.

"Go ahead," Rachel said.

Jimmy dashed over to his uncle and proudly displayed the bass.

"You should consider entering Jimmy in the children's division of the derby," Tom said. "He's a good fisherman."

"I'm afraid with school prep to do almost every night, I don't have the time to bring him out."

"Maybe another year," Tom said. "Jimmy's welcome to join me anytime I go fishing."

"That's very kind of you," she responded. "I'm sure he'd love the chance to fish again."

Jimmy ran back to them, grinning from ear to ear. "Uncle Richard says he and Dad were twice my age before they ever caught anything this big."

"Good for you." Rachel checked her watch. "You have time to fish a little longer if you'd like."

"Yes, please."

Tom chuckled at Jimmy's politeness. After storing the boy's catch in the cooler he'd brought for that purpose, he set Jimmy up at the water's edge once more.

When Tom was satisfied Jimmy could hold his own, he sat with Rachel on her blanket to watch. "Your brother-in-law has been more amiable than I expected."

"You mean better than the tyrant I painted him as?" she asked.

He shrugged.

"He seems like a doting uncle now," Rachel said. "But this afternoon my lawyer informed me that Richard filed an appeal of the judge's ruling on his parents' will."

"Do you think that's why he's really here?"

She crossed her arms, her gaze fixed on her son. "Yes, but I hope not."

Tom regretted bringing up the subject. To relax, he allowed the peace of the scenery—red hues coloring the horizon, the scent of sea air, the gentle lap of the water on the shore—to work its magic.

"Your tech guy at the police station said the changes to my smart system settings originated from somewhere else," Rachel remarked. "Could he tell if multiple attempts were made to crack the password?"

"Now that you mention it, I asked a computer whiz I know to scour the system and give a second opinion," he answered. "I'll give Rick a call to see if he's had a chance to do it yet."

Tom walked away and made the call, then returned to Rachel and shared his friend's findings. "I think this might be good news. Rick says last Tuesday night's incident was apparently scheduled earlier in the evening by someone with a password."

"So it was Richard?" she asked. "Why didn't the police tech guy see that?"

"I don't know." He feared that Richard's tentacles on the island might reach beyond Blake Culp, but he didn't want to alarm Rachel more than she already was. "Rick confirmed what our tech guy said about there being no record of where the change originated, but Rick says that doesn't rule out the possibility that it was from your desktop. Since your in-laws' system was set up to remain logged in, it's possible Jimmy inadvertently changed the settings."

Rachel stuck her hands into her jacket pockets. "Do you think I've been worried over all this for nothing? That the childish schoolyard pranks had me seeing ghosts where there weren't any?"

"No, I don't," Tom said. "Saturday's caller was real, and it was disturbing how he talked to Jimmy."

She shuddered. "Today someone locked me in the supply closet at school. I don't believe that was accidental."

"Katy texted me that she rescued you."

Rachel chuckled. "She's such a sweetheart."

"My mom's notorious lateness turned out to be a good thing," he joked.

"It did indeed. There was hardly anyone around to hear me shouting."

"Do you have any idea who locked the door?"

"I'd just finished meeting with Blake Culp about his son," she replied. "He wasn't happy when I cautioned him that waiving Ian's probation wasn't a done deal simply because I was offering remedial work."

Tom squirmed inwardly. He didn't like the fact Blake was a longtime friend of Richard's either. He could have further tainted Blake's perception of Rachel. Tom wanted to ask if Ellen had been working at the school today, but he hesitated. He hadn't told Rachel he'd seen Ellen near the house Sunday afternoon. If Ellen wasn't the culprit, he didn't want Rachel to feel rattled whenever the woman was at the school.

"Did you see my text about the PE teacher?" Rachel asked.

"No." Tom whipped out his phone and scrolled through his messages. How had he missed that? He read the text. "Did you see Trent Davis at the school before you went into the supply closet?"

"No, I didn't," she said. "I haven't officially met him yet, but I know what he looks like."

"I'll have a chat with him tomorrow anyway," he assured her.

"I can't imagine why Trent would want to frighten Jimmy," Rachel mused. "Although it was more likely a student, rather than Trent, who dropped the notepaper you found. The PE teacher probably gave similar workout regimens to several of his students. Unfortunately, a student might think calling my house and frightening my son was as harmless a prank as pulling up stakes in the garden or hiding my bulletin board."

"Trent should be able to tell me the names of every student he gave workout papers to," Tom said.

Richard glanced over his shoulder at them.

Tom wondered if he could hear their conversation.

Rachel eyed Richard warily and lowered her voice, as if she'd had the same thought. "I know my caller ID listed Saturday's call as private, but is it possible for the police to get the number from the phone company?"

"I already tried," he said. "The call came from an unregistered cell phone."

"A burner phone?"

"Unfortunately, yes," Tom replied. Many people owned pay-as-you-go phones and opted not to register them, but criminals of every stripe were known for using them precisely because they couldn't be tracked. "If we find a viable suspect, I could get a warrant to check his phone for a record of an outgoing call to your number."

She continued to stare at Richard. "Interesting."

Was Rachel thinking that *she* wouldn't need a warrant? Suddenly feeling even more uneasy that Richard planned to hang around for a week, Tom hoped she wouldn't do or say anything that might alert Richard that she was suspicious of him.

If she did, Tom feared the consequences could be devastating.

9

Early the next morning, Rachel hustled Jimmy to the car so she could prep for her classes at school.

"You're leaving awfully early, aren't you?" Richard asked.

She jumped at the sound of his voice.

"Uncle Richard!" Jimmy shouted.

"Hey, champ." Richard held up a tray with two steaming cups and a paper bag from the local café. "I brought coffee and muffins."

Surprised by his early appearance, Rachel fumbled Jimmy's lunch bag. "Thanks. That was really nice of you. But I'm afraid I have to get to school to do prep work I didn't have time to do yesterday."

"Can Uncle Richard drive me later?" Jimmy asked.

Before Rachel could protest, Richard said, "Sure, I'd be happy to do that."

Jimmy jumped up and down.

She tensed. "I don't think that's a good idea." What was Richard trying to do? He had to have an ulterior motive for suddenly playing nice after more than two months of estrangement. But what did he hope securing Jimmy's affection would do for him? Her heart pinched. He couldn't be thinking of kidnapping his own nephew. He'd never get away with it.

"Please," Jimmy begged her.

"I promise I'll get him to school on time," Richard added.

With a heavy sigh, Rachel reluctantly agreed. How could she refuse without sounding paranoid? She dug around in her purse for her spare key and gave it to Richard, then got Jimmy's booster seat out of the car. "He needs to be at school no later than eight thirty." School didn't start until nine, but she wanted to make sure Jimmy was there in plenty of time.

"No problem," Richard assured her.

Rachel hugged Jimmy goodbye. "Be good for your uncle."

"I will," Jimmy said.

Richard handed her a cup of coffee and the paper bag. "You might as well take these to go."

"Thank you." For a fleeting second, his amiable smile reminded her of James's. She shook away the errant thought. James never would have treated them the way Richard had these past two months.

As Rachel pulled out of the driveway, she glanced toward Tom's place. The driveway was empty. He had probably gone to work early too. Her stomach churned at the realization that she'd subconsciously hoped that at least Tom would be around to keep an eye on Richard.

By the time she reached the school, her overactive imagination had worked her into a frenzy. She called Tom and explained the situation. "If you're out patrolling, could you drive by my house and make sure Richard has left for school with Jimmy?"

"Absolutely," he said.

The churning in her gut eased. Rachel thanked him and disconnected.

The next hour flew by. Before she knew it, students began arriving. She checked the clock every few minutes. When eight thirty came with no sign of Jimmy, the churning in her gut resumed with a vengeance. She grabbed her phone to call Tom as a text alert sounded.

Richard and Jimmy are on their way, Tom texted. *I'm tailing them to make sure they don't detour.*

Her insides melted at the news. Rachel replied with heartfelt gratitude.

Fifteen minutes later, Richard appeared at her classroom door with Jimmy and his booster seat. "I'm sorry we're late. I lost track of time."

"We had so much fun," Jimmy interjected. He told her about the beanbag toss game he'd played with Richard.

Clearly, her son had missed having his uncle around. Boys needed a father figure in their lives, and now Richard was the only one Jimmy had.

Her thoughts flashed to Tom teaching Jimmy to fish last night, and her heart somersaulted. Pushing the thought aside, Rachel said to Richard, "Thank you for taking such good care of him. I'd better escort him to his class now. The bell is going to ring soon." She said goodbye to Richard without making plans for when they'd see him next.

After ensuring Jimmy was safely delivered to school, Tom decided to take the opportunity to speak to the PE teacher about his training note. He strode to the office and asked to see Trent Davis.

"Sign in, please," the secretary said.

After he did so, the secretary directed him to Trent's office.

Tom walked down the hall and knocked on Trent's open door.

Trent sat behind his desk. He glanced up from his computer and motioned for Tom to enter. "Have a seat."

Tom obliged, then introduced himself and briefly explained the reason for his visit.

"I wrote out customized exercise regimens for all my students at the end of last year," Trent said.

Tom showed him a picture he'd snapped on his cell phone of the page he'd found in the garden. "Can you tell me whose list this was?"

"It's one I goofed on and discarded. The chart is half-done."

Tom frowned. He doubted a student would pilfer a discarded page from the trash and deliberately plant it to frame the teacher. Besides, Trent had prepared the sheets at the end of the last school year, and the trash cans had long since been emptied. "How do you feel about the school's newest teacher?" Tom asked.

Trent leaned back in his chair. "I haven't met her yet."

Tom couldn't detect any deception or anxiety in the teacher's response and relegated the would-be clue to the unrelated pile. He thanked Trent for his time, then stopped by Rachel's class before he left. He told her about his conversation with Trent.

"Thank you so much for watching out for Jimmy this morning," she said, not seeming to even register what he'd said about the PE teacher. "I was a basket case worrying about him. And it seems silly now. Jimmy loved his time with his uncle."

"But you still don't trust Richard?" he asked.

"Not really," Rachel admitted. "He hasn't said anything about his parents' will since he got to the island, so I can't help but see everything he does as somehow connected to his latest appeal of the will."

"Try not to worry," Tom said. "Things have a way of working out."

She gave a grim look and disappeared into her classroom as the bell rang.

At lunchtime, Principal Bruce Sutton summoned Rachel to the cafeteria, not as a teacher but as a parent. The tables and floor were littered with tossed food and wrappings, and Jimmy stood at the end of one table next to the lunchroom monitor.

Mr. Sutton was in his early forties, and he wore a suit and tie as usual.

"Sally Peters claims Jimmy started a food fight," he informed Rachel.

"Is this true?" Rachel asked her son.

"No," Jimmy insisted.

"Were you throwing food?" Rachel asked.

Jimmy ducked his head. "Yes." Then he raised his chin. "But I didn't start it."

Rachel believed her son. She'd caught him in enough lies over the years that she knew when he was telling the truth. "You know that throwing food is wrong, wasteful, and against the rules."

Jimmy seemed to deflate. "Yes."

"You need to stay in from recess to help clean up the mess," Rachel instructed him.

Jimmy set to work, but to Rachel's surprise and disappointment, none of the other children involved in the food fight were required to stay behind and help too. She understood how the principal wouldn't want to appear to show favoritism to the son of a teacher and therefore took the tattletale at her word, but clearly Jimmy hadn't been alone in causing the mess.

Principal Sutton slipped away before Rachel could express her frustration with the unbalanced treatment of her son.

Jack arrived with a mop and bucket on wheels, appearing tired. For the first time, Rachel noticed the arthritic malformation on several of his knuckles.

Rachel helped Jimmy pick up and dispose of all the retrievable pieces of waste. Before they left for class, she told Jimmy he needed to apologize to the custodian for making more work for him.

"I'm sorry," Jimmy told him.

Jack seemed slightly embarrassed by the apology. "I appreciate you staying behind to help me clean the floor."

As Rachel walked Jimmy to his classroom, he reiterated that he hadn't started the food fight and didn't know why Sally said he had.

"When you do things you shouldn't, you open yourself up to being blamed for worse things," Rachel said. "I hope you'll remember that the next time you're tempted to participate in something you know is wrong."

"I will," he promised. "I'm sorry."

Thankfully, Rachel's afternoon classes unfolded without any more unwelcome surprises.

At the end of the school day, she invited Ian to her desk to give him a written summary of the agreement they'd come to concerning his probation waiver—Ian could play football again, but he had to continue his remedial work. If his grades hadn't shown a notable improvement within a month, he wouldn't be able to play again. When she tugged the agreement from her book bag, a small piece of paper drifted to the floor.

Ian stooped down and retrieved it for her. He squinted at the words and sounded out gibberish in his attempt to read it.

Rachel took the note from him and scanned it. Ignoring the galloping thud in her chest, she stilled her trembling hand and did her best not to show the note's effect on her.

"What does it say?" he asked.

She studied the letters to make sense of Ian's thoroughly backward phonetic attempt to read it. "Oh!" she exclaimed, realizing that reading it backward was exactly what he'd been doing. Excitement welled inside her at the revelation.

Rachel hurried to her filing cabinet in the corner of the room and pulled out a folder of paragraphs at various reading levels in a special typeface that was easier for dyslexics to read. Choosing one at a grade seven reading level, she presented it to Ian and asked him to read it aloud.

Ian read it with relative ease, which corroborated her theory. She'd suspected a form of dyslexia might be one of his problems when she'd seen his trouble with spelling, although there'd been no telltale letter reversal in his work. She thought his remedial teacher in grade school would have picked up on the problem.

"Has anyone ever told you that you're dyslexic?" Rachel asked.

Ian shook his head, looking ashamed.

"It's not your fault. You just process what you see differently from other people." She explained how the condition could manifest.

"Yeah, the letters and numbers bounce around too," he said. "You mean that's not what they do for everybody?"

"No," Rachel answered. "Now that we better understand what you're struggling with, we can use various typefaces and other resources to make it easier for you to read. You're obviously very smart to have done as well as you have when the words on the page are doing crazy gymnastics in front of your eyes."

Ian seemed to grow two inches at her praise, and she suspected no one had ever complimented him on his intelligence before. At least, not since those early primary school teachers who had recognized his brightness, despite his lack of attention to bookwork.

"Give me a few days to gather the resources, but I should have them put together by week's end," Rachel said. "I'm confident they'll help make reading and writing much easier for you."

Ian beamed at the news and thanked her repeatedly as he left.

Rachel wished his elation were contagious. But as she stuffed the note he'd retrieved back into her book bag, its words burned into her mind.

You don't belong here.

10

"We're going to stop by the police station on the way home," Rachel said to Jimmy as she took a detour from her usual route. Whoever didn't want her here was in the school and near Jimmy. He'd already frightened her son over the phone, so what else was he capable of?

Jimmy bounded out of the car when they arrived. He motioned across the parking lot. "Can I go see the police dog?"

Rachel walked Jimmy across the lot to the K-9 officer. "Could my son meet your dog?"

The officer smiled. "Sure thing. This is Bruiser," he said to Jimmy and signaled the dog to sit. "You can pet him."

Bruiser had a square, well-muscled build and carried his head as if proud to be an officer. The dog stood about a foot shorter than Jimmy, but he was probably double his weight.

"Is he a German shepherd?" Jimmy asked.

"No, he's a Belgian Malinois."

"I don't think I've ever heard of that breed before," Rachel said.

"They're great dogs," the officer said. "Good with kids if they're raised with them. They're also protective and outgoing, but they're very active. They're not for the couch potato."

Rachel laughed and petted the dog. A protective dog around the house would be nice, but with them at school all day, it wouldn't be fair to the animal.

Tom drove into the parking lot in his cruiser and parked near them. "What brings you here?" he asked Rachel. "Is there a problem?"

Rachel stepped away from the other officer, who was now showing Jimmy the commands he used with Bruiser. She drew the note from her purse, holding it by the corner, and passed it to Tom. "I'm hoping you can dust this for fingerprints or something."

Before taking the note from her, he slipped on a pair of latex gloves. "Where did you find it?"

"My book bag. Well, Ian Culp noticed it first. I was meeting with him after school to do some assessments, and the note fell out of my bag when I pulled out a book." She wrung her hands, but she couldn't stop them from trembling. "Whoever scared Jimmy on the phone Saturday afternoon clearly has no intention of stopping."

"Could Ian have put the note in your bag?" Tom asked. "Or maybe he only pretended to find it?"

"I don't think so. He couldn't even read it." Rachel explained how she'd discovered the teen was dyslexic.

Tom turned to the other officer. "Can you keep an eye on Jimmy here for a few minutes? I need to check something with his mother inside."

"Sure thing."

Once inside, Tom dusted the note for fingerprints and found two sets. He took Rachel's prints to eliminate hers, leaving one set.

"They must be Ian's prints because he handed me the note with his bare hands." Rachel shook her head. "But I can't believe he wrote it. Why would he?"

"The perpetrator likely knows I'm investigating previous incidents, so he or she might have worn gloves," he said. "Was Ellen Donovan working today?"

"You still think Ellen could be behind this? That she said those awful things to Jimmy over the phone?"

"I don't know," Tom admitted. "But I saw her driving slowly by your place the next afternoon."

"And you didn't tell me?" Rachel asked, her voice hitting a new pitch. She couldn't believe that Tom had kept this from her. Ellen was often in the school, so she could reach Jimmy anytime. Had she coaxed that girl to blame Jimmy for the food fight?

"I had a little chat with her, and I wasn't convinced she was the culprit," he said. "I figured if she were behind it, the fact I was on to her would spook her from doing anything else."

"Clearly, it hasn't."

"If she's our culprit, which we don't know for sure," Tom reminded her.

"She was at the school today." Rachel sucked in a deep breath and forced herself to calm down. "She could have snuck into my classroom while I was on recess duty or at lunch."

"I'll talk to her again," he said, then escorted Rachel back outside.

At the sight of her son hanging on the officer's every word, another possible perpetrator occurred to Rachel. She caught Tom's arm to stop him before they reached Jimmy and lowered her voice. "Maybe Richard slipped the note into my bag when he came into the classroom this morning. Or when he stopped by the house first thing."

It seemed more than plausible. Rachel already knew her brother-in-law didn't want her to stay here.

But how far would he go to force her to leave?

Tom arrived home at dinnertime and noticed the lights on at Rachel's house, but there was no sign of her car. Concerned someone had broken in, he sneaked over to her cottage and peeked into every first-floor window. Through the kitchen window, he spotted a pair of legs sticking out from beneath the sink.

He removed his phone from his pocket and texted Rachel. *Did you hire a plumber?*

She responded immediately. *No. Why?*

Don't sweat it. I'll check it out. Tom slid the phone into his pocket, then tried the kitchen door. It was unlocked, so he quietly let himself in. "What do you think you're doing?" he barked.

The man banged his head as he attempted to sit up, then slid out from beneath the sink. He held a monkey wrench in one hand and rubbed his head with the other. "Fixing a clogged drain."

Tom was startled to see Richard. "I texted Rachel, and she didn't know anything about you fixing her plumbing."

"I wanted to surprise her," Richard said. "I noticed a few minor maintenance issues when I was watching Jimmy this morning. I also repaired a couple of squeaky doors, serviced the furnace, and caulked the bathroom sink."

After learning that Richard had been doing his utmost to oust her from the place, Tom wasn't ready to believe the man had Rachel's best interests at heart. "How did you get inside?"

Richard pointed the monkey wrench toward a key on the counter, then tossed the wrench into an ancient toolbox. "I forgot to give Rachel her key when I dropped Jimmy off this morning." He checked his watch. "I thought she'd be home by now. Did she have something going on at school?"

"I'm not sure where she is." Tom crossed his arms, trying to decide if Richard was genuinely being nice or merely proactive about getting the house ready to sell after he managed to kick Rachel out.

Richard sighed. "From that scowl, I'm guessing she told you I appealed my parents' will."

Tom nodded.

Richard snapped the toolbox shut and returned it to a shelf in the mudroom. "I'd better be going. I still want to get some fishing in. Can you give Rachel her key back?"

"Sure." Tom accepted the key from him.

Richard clasped the doorknob and paused. "For the record, the repairs were for Rachel's benefit. No ulterior motive."

Tom doubted that. The man was a lawyer. Every word, every action was most likely calculated.

As Richard crossed the yard to the cottage he'd rented, Tom glanced around the house, but he saw no evidence Richard had done anything more than he'd claimed. Tom texted Rachel to let her know that Richard had been playing Mr. Handyman.

I wasn't expecting that, she replied.

Tom locked the house and pocketed Rachel's key, then texted her again. *He gave me your key to return to you. I guess he figured letting himself in uninvited—even to do a good deed—wasn't a great idea when you have a suspicious cop living next door.*

Thanks for checking on the place for me.

Anytime, neighbor.

Tom went home and heated leftovers for his dinner. He tried to read the newspaper as he ate, but he couldn't stop thinking about Richard. What had he really been up to in Rachel's house?

He itched to text Rachel again and ask where she was, but it was none of his business. When she got home, Tom would hand over her key, and he'd feel better if he could rule out a couple of suspicions before then. He loaded his dishes into the dishwasher and drove to the police station to borrow their high-sensitivity meter for radio frequencies. By the time he returned, Rachel still wasn't home.

Tom had a key. Should he let himself in and sweep the place without asking permission? He was sure she wouldn't mind, and he'd rather not add to her concerns if his suspicions turned out to be nothing. Besides, she'd probably prefer he run his tests while Jimmy wasn't around to see and potentially report Tom's actions to his uncle.

Leaving his truck at his own house, Tom walked to Rachel's and let himself in, then combed the premises from top to bottom for listening devices or any type of spy equipment that might be transmitting a signal out of the house. Richard's rental house was in an ideal location to intercept such signals, which could be another reason why he chose to stay nearby.

Half an hour later, Tom finished his sweep. He'd found nothing. Spotting Rachel's car pulling into the driveway, he hurried outside so she wouldn't worry over seeing lights on in her house.

Her headlights swept over him, and the vehicle came to an abrupt halt. She jumped out. "What's going on?"

"Nothing to worry about." Tom told her he'd gotten suspicious of what else Richard might have been up to inside, but he'd found no evidence that was the case. "It seems your brother-in-law has had a change of heart."

Rachel sent Jimmy inside to get ready for bed. "I wish I could be as confident as you are. The truth is, I took Jimmy out to dinner because I didn't want to face Richard, especially after finding the note at school."

Tom's heart ached at the anguish in her voice. "That's understandable."

"Maybe, but it's not fair to Jimmy. He adores his uncle. And apparently Richard has come here to spend time with him."

"Gut instincts shouldn't be ignored." Tom removed her key from his pocket and handed it to her. "Richard asked me to give you this."

She frowned at it. "I'm not usually so distrustful, but I can't help feeling his giving the key to you was just a way to take suspicion off himself. He could have easily made a copy."

"There's a quick way to alleviate that concern," he said. "I can simply have the locks rekeyed. I'll take care of it tonight."

"Do you think I'm being paranoid?"

"Not at all. Your concerns are justified. And for the record, from the way my sister gushes about your class, she thinks you're the best teacher ever, so you most definitely belong here."

Rachel smiled. "Thank you."

But clearly someone on this island didn't think Rachel belonged here. Tom needed to figure out who it was before it was too late.

11

Thursday morning, Tom slowed his early morning run to a trot as he neared Rachel's house. Her car was already gone, and he'd spotted Richard driving toward the beach at dawn, likely to get in more fishing. How long would that occupy him?

When Tom returned home, he showered and dressed in jeans and a T-shirt.

He hadn't seen Rachel the previous day. He'd responded to a domestic disturbance call that had become a long and tense standoff. And her brief reply text to his inquiry about her day had left him wondering if she was holding something back. What if she was so worried about appearing paranoid that she failed to alert him to someone who could prove to be a real danger?

At least Tom didn't have to work today, so he could watch for trouble. But he didn't know where. At her house? Or at the school?

When his cell phone chirped with his mother's ringtone, Tom grabbed the phone. "What's up?"

"My car won't start. Can you drive Katy to school?"

"I'll be right there." He put on a windbreaker, then snagged a protein bar and a water bottle on his way out the door. He'd been meaning to volunteer at the school more often, and hanging out there today would give him the opportunity to keep an eye out for any other strange incidents involving Rachel.

As soon as Tom pulled up in front of his mom's house, Katy bounded out. He couldn't help chuckling at how enthusiastic she was about school. Then again, if he'd had a teacher like Rachel, maybe he would have been excited about school too.

Tom shook his head. Rachel was a victim of harassment, and he'd been the responding officer. Thinking of her as anything else at this point wasn't wise or ethical.

He drove to the school, noting Rachel's car parked in the section for teachers, and walked Katy to her classroom.

"Good morning," Rachel said to Tom as if genuinely happy to see him.

"Is it?" Tom whispered. "Have you had any other incidents?"

"No, but thank you for asking."

"Did you see Richard yesterday?"

"Actually, I haven't seen or heard from him since he dropped Jimmy off here Tuesday morning," she responded. "I feel like I should invite him over for dinner. Jimmy's been asking about him, and Richard seems to have taken the first step toward reconciliation."

"I spotted him heading to the beach this morning when I was on my run." He didn't know if she was asking his opinion, but he refrained from voicing one. Richard made him uneasy, but he was Jimmy's uncle.

"I thought the fishing derby might be keeping him busy," Rachel said. "Have you been out fishing again?"

"Not yet." Normally, Tom would already be out on the water, given this was his day off, but he couldn't kick this compulsion to look out for his new neighbor. Katy would be heartbroken if her teacher left or anything happened to her. But privately he had to admit that he wasn't doing it only for his sister's sake. Rachel was becoming more important to him, and he wanted to keep her safe. "I'm volunteering at the school today."

"It's your day off and you're not fishing?" she asked, surprise evident in her voice.

"I wouldn't say that." He winked. "I'm angling to hook a different kind of slippery cold-blooded creature."

Rachel shivered, clearly catching his meaning, and gave him a grateful smile.

The bell rang, and Tom excused himself.

The volunteer coordinator put him to work assessing the playground and sports equipment for safety hazards. The task allowed him to watch the outside door to Rachel's classroom. Unfortunately, he missed out on sharing lunch with her because his mother needed a ride to the bank and her knitting class.

"I'm sorry to be so much trouble," his mom said.

"It's no problem." Tom parked in front of the bank. He spotted Richard going into the building and unbuckled his seat belt. "I needed to come here today anyway." He followed his mother up the sidewalk and held the door for her.

Richard was speaking to one of the tellers.

Tom stepped into line behind his mother, where he could also watch Richard. Tom's first thought had been that Richard was visiting the bank concerning his parents' estate. If that was the case, he would need to meet with a bank associate in his or her office, not a teller. Since Richard didn't live on the island, Tom doubted the man had his own account here. So, if he was simply withdrawing cash, why not use the ATM?

The teller left the wicket. A moment later, she returned with a large stack of bills, which she counted in front of Richard. There must have been several hundred dollars in the stack. Richard stuffed the money into a white business-size envelope, then slipped the envelope into the inside pocket of his jacket.

"Sir," a teller called.

The elderly lady behind Tom gave him a gentle nudge. "She's talking to you."

Tom glanced at the available teller, then back at Richard, who was now exiting the bank.

His mother closed her purse as she walked over to Tom. "I'll wait for you outside."

"That's okay. We can go now. I, uh, remembered something else I need to do." Tom ushered her back to his truck. He slid behind the wheel, watching the direction Richard turned at the end of the street. With any luck, Tom would be able to pick up his trail after dropping his mother at her class.

"You go on," his mom said. "I'll walk to my class."

"Are you sure?"

"Yes. It's a beautiful day for a stroll."

Tom's attention strayed to the street once more.

"Go get your man," she said.

He gaped at her.

His mom laughed. "I saw you eyeballing him in the bank. I know your cop face when I see it."

Tom gave her a quick hug. After she got out of the truck, he sped off in time to spot Richard disappearing around a corner. Tom followed, staying several car lengths behind him so the man wouldn't get spooked.

As Tom drove, he considered the money Richard had withdrawn from the bank. Was it a gift for Rachel and Jimmy? Most people refrained from carrying that much cash around while vacationing. And Richard didn't strike Tom as a drug user. But Richard could use the cash to pay someone—maybe someone he'd hired to scare Rachel into moving out of the cottage.

Richard steered onto the road to Rachel's house. Tom slowed his vehicle to a crawl as he followed. Richard passed Rachel's driveway and parked at the cottage he'd rented.

Tom returned to his own house and waited to see if the man left again.

Fifteen minutes later, Richard strode across Rachel's yard to her shed. He emerged with a pair of garden shears and proceeded to trim the bushes in front of her cottage.

Deciding he was wasting his time spying on the man, Tom headed back to the school.

Rachel was teaching her class outside by the garden. She motioned him over as he exited his truck.

His pulse quickened, and he hurried over to her. "Did something happen?"

"No. I'm sorry. I didn't mean to worry you. I wanted to tell you that I heard from Richard. He agreed to come over for dinner tonight." She worried her bottom lip. "I was wondering if you might like to join us too."

"I'd like that. Thank you. What time?"

"Five thirty."

"Can I bring anything?"

"Just yourself."

Tom debated telling her about the cash he'd seen Richard withdraw from the bank. He decided to wait. If the man planned to give the money to Rachel, Tom didn't want to spoil the surprise.

After school, Rachel collected Jimmy from his classroom. Once they were settled in the car, she said, "Uncle Richard is coming for supper, so we need to stop at the general store on the way home."

"Yippee!" Jimmy shouted. "Can we go fishing again?"

"Not tonight," she said. "I don't think we'll have time for it with everything else. Don't forget you have school tomorrow."

Jimmy groaned.

As Rachel entered the parking lot for the general store, she noticed a work truck parked in front of the vegetable stand behind the store. Blake Culp's name was emblazoned on the side panel.

She scanned the area for Blake while she helped Jimmy out of the back seat. This wasn't the ideal place, but she hoped to tell him about her ideas for helping Ian cope with his dyslexia or at least set up a time to do so. Now that Ian was allowed to play football again, Blake was proving much more difficult to get in touch with.

Rachel nudged Jimmy toward the store, where she bought two packages of chicken legs for the evening's meal. They wouldn't make the fanciest home-cooked meal, but at least she could cook them quickly. With any luck, Tom would love the herb-and-Parmesan coating she baked them in as much as Jimmy did.

She usually allowed Jimmy time to roam the aisles of the general store to check out the intriguing variety of toys, but today Rachel needed to hurry home and get supper started.

They returned to the car. As Rachel helped Jimmy buckle his seat belt, she spotted Blake. She set the grocery bag on the back seat beside Jimmy. "I'll be right back. I need to have a word with someone." Rachel rounded the car and abruptly halted at the sight of Richard approaching the man.

"You'll take care of it?" Richard asked.

"Of course," Blake assured him.

"Good." Richard slapped Blake on the back and handed him an envelope. "I'm counting on you."

When Blake opened the envelope, revealing a thick stack of bills, Rachel's breath caught in her throat. What was Richard paying Blake to do?

Rachel ducked out of view. Blake was a handyman. There could be a perfectly innocent explanation for the payoff. Richard could be hiring Blake to do repairs on the cottage. But why would he pay the man cash when the expense could legitimately come out of the estate? And why wouldn't he consult her first?

She reached for her door handle, her hands shaking. She fumbled the car key, and it took her three attempts to push it into the ignition.

"What's wrong?" Jimmy asked from the back seat.

Rachel looked at him in the rearview mirror. "Nothing. Everything's fine." Her voice quavered.

Sitting straighter, she inhaled a deep breath and chided herself for jumping to conclusions. There were any number of reasons why Richard had given his old friend an envelope of cash. Maybe they had a bet on who'd catch the biggest fish today. Maybe Richard had bought a boat from Blake. Maybe he was handling the rental of the cottage.

Forcing the speculations from her mind, Rachel backed out of the parking lot and headed home. She fought the compulsion to call Tom on speaker as she drove. The last thing she needed was Jimmy overhearing the conversation and repeating it to his uncle.

But keeping her thoughts bottled inside only made them spiral into even wilder theories. Perhaps Richard was paying Blake to spook her into moving off the island. They'd ruled out Richard as a suspect in all the pranks that happened at school because he'd been working in Boston, but it was possible he'd paid Blake to put his son up to them. And Blake could have been spying on her house the day Jimmy answered the phone and been terrified by the caller, who could've been Blake or Richard if Blake had alerted him to the opportunity.

Rachel's stomach churned. The mere thought that Richard would torment his own nephew so cruelly made her physically sick.

She needed to casually mention to Richard that she'd seen him and Blake outside the general store and couldn't help noticing that he'd given his old friend some cash. Hopefully, he'd explain what happened. She was pretty good at discerning when someone was lying. Then again, Richard was a lawyer, so he probably had a lot of experience manipulating the truth to suit his ends.

"The chicken smells burned," Jimmy piped up from the back seat.

"The chicken?" Rachel sniffed. *Smoke?* She glanced from one side window to the other, wondering where the smell was coming from. As she returned her attention to the road, the smell seemed to get stronger. Smoke was coming from the dash!

"The car must be overheating," she concluded, but none of the car's warning lights were on to indicate low fluid levels or an overheated engine. She stepped on the gas as they reached their street. "Don't worry. We're almost home."

The moment Rachel parked in her driveway, a sharp pain jabbed her ankle. She jerked her foot away, and a spark danced to the floor. "What in the world?" She opened the door and jumped out of the car.

A second spark spiraled to the floor mat from under the dash.

"Get out of the car!" She yanked the floor mat from the car and smothered the flame, then scooped Jimmy out of his booster seat and hurried toward the front porch.

"You forgot the chicken!" he yelled.

Rachel set him on the porch. "Stay here." She rushed back to the car to retrieve the chicken and her book bag.

Several more sparks smoldered on the floor beneath the dash where she'd removed the floor mat. She circled to the other side of the car to avoid reaching over them.

Rachel opened the passenger door, and the sound of rushing air froze the breath in her throat.

Then the car erupted into flames.

12

At the blare of fire engine sirens, Tom steered his pickup to a stop on the side of the road to allow the trucks to pass. As he eased back into traffic, he snapped on his police radio to find out what the emergency was. With the cooler weather setting in and people starting to use their woodstoves, fires weren't uncommon, especially if the homeowner didn't take the time to clean the chimney before using it.

"Car fire," the dispatcher said and repeated an address Tom knew by heart—Rachel's.

Tom stepped on the gas. If she was already home, then chances were good she wasn't in the car when it caught fire. *Please, Lord, let that be true*, he prayed.

When he swerved onto their road, the swirl of emergency lights swept an unnerving strobe effect through the trees. But at least he couldn't see any flames.

At the sight of an ambulance parked in front of Rachel's house, its back doors yawning open and the gurney removed, Tom's heart clenched.

He parked in his own driveway and raced across the yard to Rachel's front porch. A paramedic was wrapping a bandage around Rachel's arm.

"What happened?" Tom demanded.

"I don't know," Rachel said. "The car started smoking, and then it burst into flames."

"It sounds like an electrical malfunction," the paramedic interjected, closing his kit. "My aunt had the same thing happen to her last year.

Sparks started falling on her leg from beneath the dash. Thankfully, she had a fire extinguisher in the car and was able to pull over and smother it before it could get any worse."

Tom searched Rachel's eyes. She seemed skeptical of the explanation, and so was he. If it wasn't for all the other things that had been happening to her lately, he might chalk up the incident to the engine overheating or an electrical failure, but this was too coincidental.

The fire captain and Officer Wayne Beckett joined them on the porch as the paramedic left.

Beckett appeared surprised to see Tom. "Not enough to do on your day off?"

"Mrs. Sound is my neighbor," Tom explained. "I saw the fire trucks as I was coming home."

"Ah, I see."

Tom didn't think he did. Beckett had recently returned to work after a two-week vacation. He probably hadn't heard about the troubles plaguing Rachel. Tom glanced around, unwilling to get into details with little ears around. "Where's Jimmy?"

"One of my men is showing him the inside of a fire truck," the captain replied.

"I'd like to ask you a few questions," Beckett said to Rachel. He took a notepad and a pen out of his pocket. "Were you smoking?"

"Absolutely not," Rachel answered, sounding affronted by the suggestion.

Beckett scribbled on his notepad. "When did you first notice the problem?"

"A little before I turned onto my road," she said. "None of the warning lights were on, so I assumed I could make it home. But as soon as I parked, sparks started dropping on the floor from under the dash."

Beckett faced the captain. "It doesn't sound like an overheated radiator."

"It seems more likely that something shorted in the electrical system," the captain said.

"Do things like that happen accidentally?" Rachel asked, sounding terrified.

"They can," the captain said.

As the captain continued to speak with Rachel, Tom pulled Beckett aside so he could talk to him privately. "I'm concerned this might be a case of sabotage. Mrs. Sound has been the victim of a number of incidents lately."

Beckett raised his eyebrows. "Do you know who's behind them?"

"I have some ideas," Tom answered. "But I don't have any definitive suspects."

Beckett nodded. "We can tow the car in and give it a thorough examination."

"Thanks," Tom said. "I'd appreciate it."

Tom and Beckett rejoined Rachel and the captain.

"We're going to figure out what happened," Tom said as he knelt down next to Rachel. "I promise you."

Rachel swallowed audibly. "Thank you."

"Did you notice anything out of the ordinary inside the car when you got in?" Beckett asked her.

"No, I was rushing to the store after school to pick up chicken for tonight's supper." She stared at her destroyed car, lips trembling. "The chicken's still in the back seat."

The captain shook his head. "I'm afraid it won't be edible now."

"Maybe I should call Richard and postpone tonight's dinner plans," Rachel said.

A firefighter interrupted to ask the captain a question. The captain assured Rachel they'd clear out as soon as possible and excused himself.

Rachel ran a fingertip over the gauze the paramedic had taped over her arm. "He was at the store," she whispered.

"Who was at the store?" Tom asked.

"Richard," she replied. "I saw him hand an envelope of cash to Blake Culp."

Tom instinctively squeezed her hand.

Beckett frowned with his pencil poised over his notepad. "Do you think these men had something to do with the fire?"

"I don't know," Rachel said. "Maybe."

Tom tamped down the irritation building inside him and addressed Beckett. "I'll fill you in on potential suspects if and when forensics determines the fire wasn't an accident." He pointedly shifted his gaze to Jimmy being escorted back to the house by a friendly firefighter.

"Of course." Beckett closed the notepad. "I'll be in touch."

When Beckett had walked away, Tom returned his attention to Rachel. "Did you see any puddles left behind as you exited the parking lot at the school or the store? Or when you left home this morning?"

"Not that I noticed," Rachel answered.

"Was Ellen at school?" he asked. "Or at the store?"

"No, I didn't see her at all today."

Jimmy ran over to his mother, and she drew him onto her lap for a hug.

"I'm hungry," Jimmy said. "When are we going to eat? Is Uncle Richard still coming?"

"I don't think—"

"Don't cancel," Tom interjected.

Rachel winced.

"I'm sorry. I realize you must be exhausted. But I'd like to see Richard's reaction to all of this." Tom pushed to his feet. "You go inside with Jimmy and try to rest. I have burgers in the freezer I can throw on the grill for all of us."

"You don't have to do that," Rachel said.

"I want to," he insisted. "I just need to speak to Beckett first."

Standing at the living room window, Rachel hugged herself as she watched her scorched car being rolled onto a flatbed truck. The tension in her stomach eased a fraction at the sight of Tom supervising the entire operation. She probably shouldn't let herself lean on him, but the fire had left her more rattled than ever. She was also still shaken by seeing Richard give money to Blake Culp less than twenty minutes before the fire. The two events had to be connected. But how?

She shivered. No matter how Richard felt about her, surely he wouldn't risk Jimmy's life. Jimmy was his late brother's son. His twin brother at that. Jimmy was the spitting image of his father and uncle at his age. He was Richard's sole remaining blood relative. That bond had to be stronger than possessing a house on Martha's Vineyard.

Wasn't it?

"Why are you crying?" Jimmy asked as he tugged on Rachel's sweater.

With the back of her hand, Rachel swiped at the tears dripping down her cheeks, then knelt down and drew Jimmy into her arms. "They're happy tears. I'm so thankful the Lord brought us home in time and kept us safe."

"Except for your arm," Jimmy reminded her.

She smiled. "It's not so bad. And it reminds me how much worse it could have been."

"Like when Grandma and Grandpa died."

Rachel choked down a sob and hugged him tightly. "Yes, like that."

The flatbed truck roared to life, and Jimmy pulled away to watch it drive off.

Richard's SUV swerved into the driveway a moment later.

Jimmy dashed for the front door. "Uncle Richard's here!"

"Wait on the porch until his vehicle is off," Rachel reminded him. Her legs felt encased in cement, and as much as she tried, she couldn't make herself move from the window to greet him.

Besides Jimmy, Richard was all the family she had left in the world. Granted, the connection was tenuous, only by marriage, but he and his brother had always been so close. James's love for her had to count for something. Hugging herself once more, she closed her eyes. *Please, Lord, let my suspicions about Richard be wrong. For Jimmy's sake.*

When she opened her eyes, Richard was swinging Jimmy high in the air. Her son giggled, obviously ecstatic. Tom looked on, his expression neutral.

Richard set Jimmy down, and Tom said a few words to Richard.

Overcoming her frozen state, Rachel lurched toward the door, desperate to catch Richard's reaction. The instant she stepped outside, Richard hurried toward her.

"Tom said you were burned." Richard caught her hands and examined them. "Are you all right?"

"A minor burn on my forearm," Rachel said as she slipped her hands from his grip. "Nothing serious."

"I'm so sorry," Richard said. "I understand if you want to skip dinner tonight. Or perhaps I could go pick something up for us."

"No problem," Tom chimed in. "I've already volunteered to grill some burgers."

"Sounds great. Thanks for taking care of it," Richard commended as if he meant every word.

Jimmy dragged his uncle into the backyard to kick around his soccer ball.

"What do you think?" Rachel whispered after Richard disappeared around the corner of the house.

"He seemed angry when he heard what happened," Tom answered. "I have to admit I wondered if he was angry things didn't turn out the way he'd expected. But then his face lit up when Jimmy ran out to greet him." He shook his head. "It's hard to imagine he could fake that kind of affection."

She sighed. "I want to believe that he would never hurt Jimmy. Do you think I should come right out and ask him what he paid Blake for?"

"Hold off a bit," he advised. "Maybe he'll tell you tonight, so you won't have to reveal what you already know."

"Good point," Rachel said. "I'd better go outside and make sure Jimmy's okay. Then I'll get the fixings for the burgers ready. I have a tossed salad and potato salad we can eat with them."

"Sounds perfect," Tom said. "I'll go home and fetch the burgers."

After he left, Rachel walked into the backyard. Her heart squeezed at the precious sound of Jimmy's laughter. He was missing out on so much without his dad around or his uncle close by. Could that be why Richard hadn't wanted her to take the cottage? Because he wanted her to stay in Boston where he could see Jimmy regularly? If that was what he wanted, he had a strange way of showing it.

She watched Jimmy play with Richard until Tom returned with the burgers. While Tom grilled the meat, Rachel went into the kitchen to prepare the rest of the food and make a pitcher of lemonade.

Soon they all sat down at the picnic table in the backyard and dug into their meals.

"I'd forgotten how much I miss days like this," Richard commented, polishing off his burger.

Rachel groaned.

"Minus the car fire," Richard added.

She let out a sardonic laugh, then took a sip of lemonade.

"What happens to Jimmy if something happens to you?" Richard asked.

Rachel nearly choked on her lemonade.

"Is that a threat?" Tom demanded.

Jimmy whimpered.

"Of course not," Richard said. "I only wanted to know if Rachel had given any thought to Jimmy's care if the unthinkable happened."

She didn't know how to respond.

Richard tilted his head. "Have you written a new will? When I helped you and James draw up your wills after Jimmy was born, you made Mom and Dad his guardians if something happened to both of you. Now that they're gone, I wondered if you'd chosen a new guardian." He shrugged. "I could make the change for you if you want."

Rachel cringed. Considering how he'd been using his lawyer skills to kick her out of his parents' cottage for the past couple of months, she couldn't believe he seriously thought she'd immediately accept his offer. "I'll think about it," she said softly.

"I'd be happy to be Jimmy's guardian," Richard continued. "Without an updated will, the courts would consider me first, but if there's a couple you trust—"

"Can we stop talking about this for now?" Rachel shot a meaningful glance in Jimmy's direction. What would happen to him following her death was the last thing the six-year-old needed to be worrying about.

Richard nodded. "It's just that things happen. Like this car business. And if you lived in Boston, I could help you out. With you so far away, it's tougher."

"She has plenty of friends on the island who are more than willing to help her out," Tom said.

"Glad to hear it." Richard excused himself and went into the house to use the bathroom.

Rachel rose to begin clearing the table and noticed Richard's cell phone peeking out of the pocket of his jacket that he'd left folded across the picnic table bench. She'd told herself that if she got the chance, she'd check his phone for a record of a call to her number last Saturday afternoon. She sat where Richard had been sitting and slipped his phone from his pocket, being careful to keep it out of Jimmy's view.

"Why are you sitting in Uncle Richard's spot?" Jimmy asked.

Her hopes instantly deflated. The phone was password protected, and even if she managed to guess his password before he returned, she couldn't risk Jimmy noticing her with Richard's phone. The boy was incapable of keeping secrets. She tucked the phone back into the jacket pocket and palmed a soiled napkin that had fallen to the ground. "I was picking up some garbage." She showed Jimmy the paper napkin, then finished clearing the table.

When Richard returned, Rachel served bowls of chocolate ice cream for dessert. She kept hoping the conversation would somehow reveal why Richard had given Blake the money, but the subject never came up.

Rachel announced it was time for Jimmy to get ready for bed.

Richard hugged his nephew and promised to drive Rachel and Jimmy to school the next morning, then took his leave.

Tom hung back long enough to speak to her alone. "I'll get the report on your car as soon as the forensics team is done and let you know what they find."

"Do you think I should ask Blake what Richard hired him to do?"

"I'll speak to Blake," he said. "I don't want to tip off Richard that we're on to him if he turns out to be up to his neck in this."

She shivered. "I hope he isn't."

"Me too," Tom said. "For Jimmy's sake. That boy loves his uncle."

Rachel ushered him to the door and thanked him again for all his help.

Tom's smile reached his expressive blue eyes, making tiny creases at the corners.

They gazed at each other for a long moment. Neither of them seemed in a hurry to say good night.

"I'm done brushing my teeth!" Jimmy yelled from the top of the stairs, breaking the spell.

"I'll be right there," she called up to him.

Tom chuckled. "Sleep well." He touched her shoulder.

"You too," Rachel said as his touch electrified her senses. She immediately chided herself. Someone wanted her off the island. Now was not the time to feel such a strong connection to Tom. Never mind how safe she felt knowing he was close by.

After he left, she went upstairs and read Jimmy a book, then tucked him into bed.

Rachel ignored the school prep that needed to be done and instead searched the Internet for common causes of car fires. As she learned about electrical shorts, fuel system leaks, and faulty catalytic converters, she started to feel more at ease. Maybe the fire had been an accident after all.

The possibility didn't stop Richard's guardian question from nagging her. Even though Rachel was irritated that he'd brought up the subject in front of Jimmy, she knew that Richard was right. She needed to choose a new guardian for her son. Richard was Jimmy's uncle, so he would be the obvious choice. But as a bachelor who worked long hours, he didn't seem like a wise choice, even without her suspicions about him. Unfortunately, not being part of a couple herself anymore, she didn't have any couple friends with whom she was close enough to ask such a huge favor.

She scrolled through her phone's contact list for ideas. When she reached Charlene Russell's name, she paused. Charlene had been her best friend since grade school, her college roommate, and the maid of honor at her wedding. She wasn't married and worked crazy hours, so she wasn't really a guardian option, but Rachel knew she could talk to Charlene about anything. If anyone could help her figure out what to do, Charlene could.

Rachel hit connect and listened to the phone ring.

Charlene answered in her usual exuberant way.

Rachel filled her in on what had been happening. "Tom promised he'd let me know as soon as he gets the report on the car, and he said he'll question Blake too."

"Sounds to me as if you're seeing a lot of Tom," Charlene teased.

"Well, that's what happens when your next-door neighbor is a police officer and you've become the target of a psycho."

"Investigating officers don't usually invite victims to church events," Charlene needled.

"That was for Jimmy." Hearing how defensive she sounded, Rachel pressed her lips together and forced the sudden memory of her reaction to Tom's touch from her thoughts. He'd simply touched her shoulder. It meant nothing.

"Of course it was," Charlene said, but she didn't sound convinced.

"I didn't call you to discuss my love life," Rachel said.

"Aha! So, you admit you're attracted to Tom."

"He's been very kind to us," Rachel conceded.

"Is he tall, dark, and handsome?" Charlene asked.

Rachel rolled her eyes. "He's devastatingly handsome. All the women in the neighborhood speed up when they see his cruiser in hopes of getting pulled over by him, so they can give him their phone number."

Charlene roared with laughter.

"Seriously, he has a big heart," Rachel said. "He volunteers at a special needs camp, his church, and his sister's school."

"Your school?"

"Yes, his sister, Katy, is one of my students."

"He sounds perfect."

"I'll be sure to introduce you to him the next time you come to visit."

"Sounds good," Charlene said. "I can be there tomorrow."

"What? Are you kidding?" Rachel was used to her friend's teasing. She hadn't expected her to drop everything and invite herself to the island.

"I'll catch the five o'clock ferry and stay for the weekend," Charlene responded. "I want to meet this new man in your life."

Rachel stifled a groan. "Haven't you been listening to anything I said? Someone is trying to spook me off the island, and I'm afraid it's Richard."

Rachel considered Richard's question about Jimmy's guardianship status again. Suddenly, she worried that her brother-in-law might realize he'd be better off with her totally out of the picture sooner rather than later.

What exactly was he capable of?

13

As promised, Richard arrived early the next morning to drive Rachel and Jimmy to school. "I'll arrange for a rental car to be waiting for you when school finishes."

"You don't have to do that," Rachel protested. "I can call."

"Nonsense," Richard said. "You'll be in classes all day, and the rental agency is on my way to today's fishing spot."

"Can I come?" Jimmy piped up from the back seat.

"No, it's a school day," Rachel reminded him.

"You can join me Saturday if it's okay with your mom," Richard said. He smiled at Rachel. "I'll ask the rental agency to deliver the car to the school and leave the keys with the secretary."

"Thank you." Rachel ducked her head, ashamed of the suspicions she'd been nursing against him.

Richard helped Jimmy from the back of his SUV and gave him a hug. "Have a good day, champ. I'll see you later."

Her heart squeezed. When Richard was being a jerk, it was easy to forget he was her husband's twin, but with Jimmy in his arms, the resemblance was hard to ignore. No matter how he might feel about her and the fact that his parents had left her their cottage, he certainly wouldn't do anything to endanger his only nephew, right?

Her phone beeped. Rachel checked the screen and saw a text from Tom. *Did you get to school okay?*

She smiled. *Yes, thanks for checking. Any news on the car?*

Not yet. Should find out something by lunchtime.

Knowing Tom was on the case made Rachel feel more at ease as she walked Jimmy to his classroom.

At lunchtime, she found a quiet corner in the staff lounge to call Tom. After four rings, the call went to voice mail.

Ellen strode into the room, and Rachel disconnected the call rather than leave a message. She hadn't seen Ellen at the general store or the school the day before, but Tom had asked about her. Rachel texted him to let him know she was on her lunch break and could talk. If he called back and Ellen was still around, Rachel would take the call outside. The less the woman knew about Rachel's business, the better.

Her phone rang, but Rachel didn't recognize the number. She was about to ignore the call when she realized it might be Tom calling from a landline, so she answered.

The caller introduced himself as the claims adjuster for her insurance company. "I have a few questions about yesterday's incident."

Rachel glanced around the room. Satisfied that Ellen was preoccupied chatting with other staff members, Rachel merely faced the window and cupped her hand around the phone to contain her voice. "Yes?"

"Have you made any changes to your vehicle recently?" the man asked. "Such as the electrical system, radio, or GPS?"

"No."

"Has anyone recently borrowed the vehicle?"

"No."

"Do you keep the vehicle locked, with the windows shut, when it is parked?"

"Yes."

"Did you notice any sign the vehicle had been broken into?"

"No."

"When was the last time you had the vehicle inspected?"

"Inspected?" she repeated.

"For example, mechanics routinely do a thirty-point inspection as part of their oil change."

"My last oil change was..." Rachel hesitated. Could the insurance company give her a hard time if she'd let too much time lapse between oil changes? "I don't quite remember. It was in the spring."

"Has the car been giving you any trouble lately?"

"Not at all," she replied. "Even when I smelled smoke, not a single warning light was on."

"Our records show you recently moved to Martha's Vineyard," the man said. "May I ask what prompted that move?"

"I don't see what business that is of yours or how it's relevant to this claim." Realizing she'd raised her voice, she peered over her shoulder to find every teacher in the room and even the custodian staring at her. "Insurance claim," she mouthed and turned back to the window.

"You'd be surprised how many people run into financial trouble after a move," the man went on, his voice icy, "and then attempt to fix their problems by making an insurance claim."

Rachel gritted her teeth. "I assure you I don't have any financial issues. I have a new teaching position on the island and live in a cottage I recently inherited from my in-laws. I'm the victim here. This isn't the first—" She caught herself before finishing the thought. Telling the claims adjuster that she'd been the victim of several recent attacks might only give him more ammunition to somehow deny her claim. She clenched her fist in a vain attempt to still the trembling in her hand and took a deep breath. "May I suggest you speak to Officer Tom Olson? He's investigating the incident."

"Olson isn't the name of the officer on the police report."

Rachel's heart fluttered. "Right, there was a second officer. I don't recall his name."

"It's Beckett. And when I spoke to him this morning, he said it still wasn't clear whether the fire was an accident or sabotage."

"That may be, but I don't see how it makes any difference to how you settle my claim."

"Don't you?"

She swallowed hard. "I do *not* appreciate your tone. I have been with this insurance company for five years, and I've faithfully paid my premiums on time. This is my first claim, and I expect to be treated as a valued customer in need of help, not a potential criminal."

"You tell them," one of the female teachers sitting in the staff lounge called out supportively.

"I apologize," the man on the line said. "Rest assured you will get the settlement you are owed. We'll be in touch." He disconnected without clarifying what he'd meant. He'd seemed to imply they owed her nothing if they could prove she sabotaged her own car.

Rachel wondered why the man was so convinced that she was attempting to defraud the insurance company. Maybe Officer Beckett had said something to make him think the fire wasn't an accident.

Filled with a sudden need to check on her son, Rachel shoved her lunch into her book bag and hurried out of the staff lounge. A moment later, she spotted Jimmy playing ball with Billy in the yard. She nodded to the nearby yard monitor and scanned the area for anyone suspicious.

Reassured that nothing appeared amiss, she returned to her classroom. But the feeling of impending dread wouldn't go away.

Tom mentally reviewed the report he'd been given on Rachel's car as he drove to the school. The tech guys had found definitive proof that someone had tampered with the electrical system, likely shorting it to spark a fire. Given the probable connection between the sabotage and Tom's case, Officer Beckett had been more than willing to hand off the investigation to him.

Tom pulled up to the parking space where he'd seen Rachel's car the day before. The space was empty.

He got out and scanned the ground. Unfortunately, the pavement wasn't the kind of surface that would provide him with footprints unless the perp had walked through mud first. Tom squinted toward the school building. The windows of two classrooms had a clear line of sight of the spot. Perhaps someone in one of those classrooms had seen someone suspicious. He'd go in and talk to the teachers assigned to those classrooms and then find Rachel and fill her in on what he'd learned.

Tom bit back a groan. He'd hoped to have more helpful news to share. As he returned to his truck to park it properly, a scrap of dark-blue cloth caught his eye. He knelt down to examine it. The fabric was a heavy woven cotton similar to that used in cargo pants, and the small swatch appeared to have been torn from whatever article of clothing or book bag it had originated from. Tom folded it into his notepad and slipped it into his pocket, then backed his truck into the spot.

As he strode toward the school's front door, he met the custodian carrying two garbage bags toward the trash receptacle.

Tom greeted Jack and asked, "How many times a day do you bring garbage out here?"

Jack shrugged. "A couple at least. Why?"

"Did you notice anyone hanging around the parking lot yesterday who shouldn't be here?"

"You mean like kids loitering?" Jack asked. "There are always a few of those."

Tom nodded. "Who was here yesterday?"

"A couple of girls."

"Do you know their names?"

"They headed inside before I got close," Jack replied. "Besides, I only get to know the troublemakers I have to clean up after."

"I hear you." Tom retrieved his notepad from his pocket and showed the man the fabric swatch. "Were any of them wearing a jacket or pants in this color?"

Jack squinted at the fabric and frowned. "I didn't pay much attention."

"Thanks for your time." Tom went inside the school and reported to the office to gain permission to question a few of the teachers.

The bell rang, signaling it was time for students and teachers to return to their classrooms following lunch.

Tom's heart kicked at the sight of Rachel, her cheeks pink from the chilly autumn air.

She spoke to one of the students entering her classroom, then hurried toward him. "Do you have news?"

"Unfortunately, it seems someone did tamper with your vehicle's electrical system," Tom answered. "I was about to question the occupants of the classrooms with a view of your parked car yesterday. If that doesn't turn up any leads, I'll head to the general store to see if the manager has security footage for yesterday afternoon."

"Thank you." Rachel fingered the bandage on her burned arm. "I'd never thought about how vulnerable I am during a regular day."

The thought of how much worse the outcome could have been made his stomach churn. He had to find this creep as soon as possible.

"The claims adjuster implied I caused the fire myself to defraud them out of the insurance money," she remarked.

Tom scowled. He understood they had a job to do, but Rachel already had all the stress she could handle without being subjected to such ridiculous suspicions. "Don't worry. I'll set them straight."

"I appreciate it," Rachel said. "Have you had a chance to talk to Blake about the money Richard paid him?"

"No. I went by his jobsite this morning, but his workers said he was off the island today buying supplies."

Her crestfallen expression bothered him more than he wanted to admit. Tom reached out to squeeze her hand, but he instantly thought better of it, given all the passing students and teachers. "We'll get this guy. Don't you worry about that."

"Thanks, Tom," Rachel said. "I wouldn't have been able to keep it together through this nearly as well if you weren't here for me."

The sound of his name on her lips did funny things to his emotions. "You're a lot stronger than you think," he said encouragingly, wishing he could pull her into a comforting embrace.

"I'd better go," she said, then followed her students into the classroom.

Tom scolded himself once again. Rachel was a victim whose case he was investigating. He couldn't forget that. Trouble happened when the lines between duty and friendship blurred. As it was, he'd probably read far too much into her words. She was scared, and it was natural that she appreciated having a cop living next door, ready to come to her aid at a moment's notice.

He was usually the one counseling other officers about professional boundaries. His reluctance to get involved in a serious relationship, given the inevitability that a future wife would want children, had always made keeping his professional distance easy. What made Rachel so different?

"May I help you?" Ellen asked, interrupting his thoughts.

Tom blinked. While he'd been daydreaming, the hall had emptied, save for Ellen. He hadn't even noticed her. Did he need any more proof where distractions got him? He cleared his throat. "Yes, perhaps you can. A teacher's car was tampered with yesterday. Did you happen to notice anyone suspicious in the parking lot?"

"I didn't work here yesterday," Ellen said. "I had an appointment off the island."

He thanked her anyway, making a mental note to verify her alibi. If it checked out, then he might be ready to eliminate her as a suspect of the other incidents once and for all.

Tom and Ellen parted ways, and he headed to the classrooms overlooking the parking lot.

He questioned the students and teachers in the two classrooms, but no one offered a single piece of useful information.

As he started to leave the second classroom, however, the teacher said, "You might want to ask Blake Culp if he saw anyone suspicious."

Tom felt his pulse ratchet up a notch. Was this the lead he'd been searching for? "Why do you say that?"

"He teaches a carpentry class here, and yesterday morning, he and his students were outside doing repairs around the school."

So Blake Culp had been at school the previous day, and later he was seen accepting cash from Richard Sound.

Tom couldn't wait to talk to him.

14

"I'm sorry, but no one dropped off car keys in the office for you," the school secretary said.

"Okay, thank you." Rachel caught Jimmy's hand and headed for the door.

Principal Sutton stepped out of his office. "Officer Olson told me that you've encountered some troubles since settling on the island."

Rachel squirmed, wishing Tom hadn't involved the principal.

"I've been impressed with your work so far," Mr. Sutton continued. "Several parents have also made favorable comments about the projects they see their teens working on for your class. I hope you won't let these unfortunate incidents dissuade you from staying on."

A couple of staff members seconded his encouragement as they passed by.

Rachel's spirits lightened. "They won't. I promise you." She smiled down at Jimmy. "We're very happy here, aren't we?"

Jimmy agreed wholeheartedly, drawing chuckles from the adults.

"Come on." Rachel squeezed his hand. "I'll call Uncle Richard to find out what time he told the rental agency to deliver the car. We might have to ask someone to give us a lift there instead."

"I can do that." Tom stepped out of the staff room as they passed.

"I didn't realize you were still here," she said.

"I've been talking to some teachers and students," Tom responded. "It's taken longer than I thought."

"Any progress?" she asked.

"I learned that Blake was here yesterday," he replied. "One of his carpentry students recalled him leaving class for a few minutes to retrieve tools from his van."

Rachel tightened her grip on Jimmy's hand. "That's good to know."

"I also ran into Blake and asked him a few questions," Tom said as he ushered them down the hall. "I'll fill you in later."

When they stepped outside, Jimmy pointed to the familiar Range Rover winking its lights at them. "Uncle Richard's here!"

Rachel hesitated, wanting to hear what else Tom had to say, but Jimmy tugged her arm. "Excuse me a moment," she said to Tom, then checked for moving cars before crossing the parking lot to Richard's SUV.

Richard rolled down his window.

"The rental agency couldn't deliver a car in time?" Rachel asked. After hearing Tom's news, she didn't want to accept another ride from Richard. "Tom offered to give us a lift there."

"No need," Richard said. "I'm leaving my SUV with you. I've already booked a flight to Boston, and I'll catch a cab home from the airport. I usually use my sports car in town anyway until the weather turns. I'll pick up the Range Rover the next time I come to visit."

"Thank you," she said. "That's very generous of you, but it's not necessary. The insurance company will—"

"Cover a cheap economy car, and you deserve better," Richard interrupted, finishing her sentence. "I insist. I only need you to drive me to the airport."

"You're leaving?" Jimmy whined. "You said we'd go fishing tomorrow."

"I'm sorry," Richard said. "But I was called back to Boston. I have urgent business with one of my clients."

Rachel scrunched her nose. It was Friday, and the soonest he'd get back to Boston was that evening. Most of his clients didn't work weekends. Why couldn't his business wait until Monday? In light of her suspicions about him, she should be relieved that he was leaving, but she hated how disappointed Jimmy was. "What really brought you to the island this week?" she asked softly.

"I told you," Richard answered. "I came to see my favorite nephew."

"You have to realize how different you've acted since you've been here compared to how you've been treating us the past couple of months," she told him. "Do you still plan to appeal the judge's decision on the will?"

"It's not personal."

"It is to me, and it is to Jimmy," Rachel said. The claims adjuster's intimations of sabotage popped into her mind along with the image of Richard handing money to Blake. Did she dare ask him why?

"We've got to go now," Richard said, "or I'll miss my flight."

Jimmy jumped into the back seat before she could protest—which reminded her that she needed to get him a new booster seat soon.

Rachel called to Tom as she rounded the vehicle to the passenger side. "Richard is going home and leaving his SUV for me to drive. I need to drop him off at the airport."

Tom's grimace didn't buoy her confidence in Richard's tale. Richard wouldn't have arranged for an ambush to be waiting for her as she left the airport, would he? Not when she had Jimmy with her.

Richard reached across the front seat and opened the passenger door for her. "Hurry up. If I miss my flight, there isn't another one until tomorrow morning."

Suppressing a sigh, Rachel climbed into the seat, trying to reassure herself that everything would be fine. Richard wouldn't try anything foolish after a police officer had witnessed her getting into his vehicle.

Richard hit the gas before she'd fastened her seat belt.

Rachel glanced over her shoulder to check that Jimmy was buckled in. Behind them, Tom pulled onto the road in the same direction they were headed. Her tension eased all the more as she watched him follow their next turn.

"When are you coming back?" Jimmy asked from the back seat.

"I'm not sure," Richard replied, snagging Rachel's attention from the side mirror. "I promise I'll call."

Rachel nodded, regretting that she hadn't gotten a chance to scroll through the call log on his phone. She took a deep breath. "I meant to ask you what you hired Blake to do."

Richard's jaw clenched. "You know about that?"

"I saw you hand him an envelope of cash," she admitted.

Richard chuckled, but rather than allay her concerns, the sound gave her a chill. "It was supposed to be a surprise."

"I'm not fond of surprises."

Richard searched her eyes for a moment, then returned his attention to the road. "I hired him to do some maintenance work at the cottage, like caulking the windows and cleaning the gutters after the leaves fall."

"It didn't cross your mind that I'd want to be informed?" Rachel asked. "How did you think I'd react to a strange man showing up at my house out of the blue?"

Richard frowned. "You're right. I didn't think about it. But I didn't want you to worry about all the autumn maintenance tasks that go along with owning a home."

She squared her shoulders. "Since I do own one now, I need to get used to taking care of such chores."

Richard didn't respond as he veered onto the road to the airport. He chatted some more with Jimmy until they reached the drop-off point. Richard shifted the vehicle into park and unbuckled his seat belt.

"The SUV shut off by itself," Rachel commented.

Richard nodded. "It's an automatic feature."

"I'm glad you warned me."

"You can disable the feature on the touch screen if you prefer." Richard handed her a smart key fob. "After you buckle up, push the button to start the engine. It'll only work if you have the smart key in the vehicle and your seat belt is fastened."

"Is there anything else I should know?" she asked, suddenly nervous about borrowing his expensive SUV.

"I filled the gas tank, so you should be good for a while," Richard answered. "The owner's manual is in the glove box. As long as you have your smart key on you, lifting the door handle will unlock the door."

Considering the recent events in her life, that feature didn't appeal to Rachel any more than a vehicle that shut itself off. What if someone tried to abduct her, and she didn't want him to be able to open the door?

"You might as well park in the lot," she suggested. "I'm sure Jimmy would like to walk you in. He enjoys watching the planes take off and land."

"Can we?" Jimmy piped up from the back seat.

"For a little while. We have some time before we meet Charlene at the ferry." Rachel tightened her grip on her purse, wishing she hadn't mentioned it in front of Richard. If he'd planned an ambush for her, now he'd be able to alert his accomplice to her delay.

"Do you have a friend coming for the weekend?" Richard asked.

"That's right."

"Glad to hear you'll have company." Richard parked and grabbed his luggage out of the back.

They walked into the tiny airport. At the gate, Richard hugged Jimmy goodbye and gave Rachel a peck on the cheek. "See you soon."

She and Jimmy walked outside to the chain-link fence where they could watch the planes take off.

"Rachel!" someone shouted from the opposite end of the tarmac.

Rachel spun around to find willowy, blonde Charlene hurrying toward them. "What are you doing here?"

"My brother flew me over in his little plane," Charlene replied. "You didn't get my text?"

"No," Rachel said, wondering how she missed her friend's message. "It's great to see you."

Charlene scooted around the gate and pulled Rachel into a hug. "Well, your timing is perfect. What are you doing here?"

"Richard needed a lift."

"He's leaving?"

"Yes, he said he has urgent business with a client in Boston."

Charlene released Rachel and gave Jimmy a hug. "I've missed you. How do you like living on an island?"

"I love it," Jimmy declared. "Everyone is nice. Our neighbor is a policeman, and he took us fishing."

Charlene lifted her gaze to Rachel and arched her eyebrows. "Fishing, huh? He sounds like a great guy."

"He is. And I have a new friend named Billy." Jimmy chattered on about different activities he'd been doing with his friends at school, then described the Grandparents' Day celebration Tom had invited them to.

After Jimmy watched a couple of planes take off, the trio headed toward the SUV.

"I can't wait to meet Tom," Charlene teased.

Tom slid out from beneath the vehicle and brushed the dust from his pants and hands. "That would be me."

"What were you doing under there?" Rachel asked, alarmed.

"Making sure everything looks as it should, and it does," Tom answered. "Who's your friend?"

Trying not to sound as flustered as she felt, Rachel made the introductions.

Charlene shook his hand. "So happy to meet you. I've heard a lot about you."

"Don't believe the rumors," Tom joked.

"Perhaps you could join us for a picnic on the beach tonight," Charlene suggested. "I love the view at sunset, and there's a shop nearby that sells fresh fish tacos. They're to die for." She smiled at Rachel. "If you don't already have dinner planned."

"No, I don't," Rachel said. "It sounds lovely."

"Maybe you could bring fishing rods," Jimmy coaxed Tom.

"I could do that," Tom replied. "If your mom is okay with it."

"Of course," Rachel said. "We'd love to have you."

"I'll meet you there," Tom said. "I'm on duty until six today."

Rachel pulled him aside and said quietly, "Thank you for making sure Richard wasn't up to any funny business in lending me his vehicle."

A muscle in Tom's jaw twitched. "He could have had another ulterior motive."

"What do you mean?" Rachel asked, a sinking feeling in the pit of her stomach.

"Land Rover supplies an app so owners can find their stolen vehicle."

"Do you think Richard will use the app to track my comings and goings?"

Tom tugged on his baseball cap and watched the plane taxi down the runway. "I don't know, but he could."

"Okay, that's good to know." Rachel walked over to the SUV and opened one of the back doors, then helped Jimmy buckle himself in.

Tom raised the rear hatch and loaded Charlene's luggage. After they arranged where to meet at the beach, he said goodbye and left.

"That was gentlemanly of him to help me with my suitcase," Charlene remarked as she hopped into the passenger seat.

Rachel slid behind the wheel. When she turned to Charlene, she noticed her friend's eyes were twinkling. She refused to take the bait.

"This is Richard's SUV, isn't it?" Charlene asked.

"Yes, he's lending it to me until I can replace my car. That's why he flew home."

"That doesn't sound like the man you—"

"I'm so glad you're here," Rachel interrupted, then shifted her gaze toward the back seat to remind Charlene of little ears.

Charlene jutted out her chin and expelled a breath, blowing her wispy bangs off her forehead. "Like I was saying, Tom seems nice."

"I can't believe you came here to meet him."

"You mentioned his name in every other sentence when you were telling me about all the peculiar situations of late," Charlene said. "A good friend would want to vet the man."

"There's nothing going on between us," Rachel insisted. "He's simply the officer investigating the incidents, and he happens to be my neighbor."

"A neighbor who took your son fishing and invited you both to a Grandparents' Day event," Charlene reminded her teasingly.

"He was only being kind. You know I'm not interested in remarrying, so you can stop whatever matchmaking ploy is going through that head of yours."

"Why aren't you interested?" Charlene asked. "It's obvious Tom cares about you."

Rachel tightened her grip on the steering wheel. "Every person I've ever loved gets taken away from me." She glanced at her son in the rearview mirror and lowered her voice. "I live in terror that Jimmy will be next." She swallowed hard, but she couldn't dislodge the growing lump in her throat. "I thank God every day for giving me Jimmy. But I don't know why He keeps punishing me."

"I can see how losing your parents so young, then James, and now your in-laws would make you feel that way," Charlene said gently. "You're grieving. But I hope you can see how He's seen you through every loss. Some might even say He's blessed you."

"Someone blew up my car," Rachel said.

"But you have a caring neighbor who's determined to catch the culprit."

"Yes, but he hasn't caught him yet," Rachel whispered. "Things keep happening. This last time he could have killed us."

"Mommy, what's wrong?" Jimmy asked, clearly sensing her anxiety, even if he couldn't make out what she'd said.

"Nothing you need to worry about," Rachel assured him. "I'm just getting used to driving this SUV. We're almost home."

"Uncle Richard said it has all the latest bells and whistles." Jimmy started humming to himself, seemingly satisfied with her answer.

Rachel reasoned her excuse wasn't an utter fabrication. And she sure wasn't used to the frightening events that had forced her to drive the vehicle in the first place.

Tom arrived at the beach and spotted Rachel, Charlene, and Jimmy sitting on a blanket in the sand. It was an ideal evening for watching the sunset over the ocean. The air was cool but still, and the gentle lap of the waves on the shore soothed the soul.

He set his cooler on the sand and spread a blanket next to theirs. When he sat down, he spied takeout boxes wrapped in a beach towel on the corner of their blanket. "Have you been here long?"

"No," Rachel said. "We didn't know what you liked, so we ordered a variety of fish and a few bowls of clam chowder."

"Sounds good." Tom opened his cooler. "I brought soft drinks and veggies and dip for munching."

Charlene retrieved paper plates and utensils from their picnic basket. When she set out the plates, she nudged Rachel over to Tom's blanket to make more room for Jimmy.

Tom grinned, aware of what she was really doing in a not-so-subtle way. He didn't mind if Rachel didn't. "The food smells delicious."

"This place is top-notch," Charlene agreed as she passed around the food. "And everything always tastes better on the beach."

Although the beach wasn't as crowded as it was in summer, quite a few locals had come out to watch the sunset. Others strolled along the pier or browsed the short row of shops. Since it was derby season, dozens of fishermen stood at the ocean's edge, trying their luck.

"I think this is what I like best about life on Martha's Vineyard." Charlene drank in the view. "People slow down long enough to appreciate the beauty of God's handiwork. I love how they applaud when the sun disappears below the horizon."

"Me too," Tom said. "I savor the sunrise while I run in the mornings. There's something about hearing birds serenade a new dawn that helps me tune out all the chatter in my head and tune in to what's most important."

"I miss my morning runs," Rachel said, sounding wistful. "But I can't leave Jimmy."

"I'll bet he'd enjoy pacing you on his bicycle." Tom winked at Jimmy. "Wouldn't you? Do you think your mom could keep up with you?"

"I don't know," Jimmy said in a teasing singsong. "I ride pretty fast."

Rachel laughed. "That's a good idea. We should try it one Saturday morning."

Tom felt a pang of anxiety over what an easy target they'd make on the deserted back roads in the early morning hours and regretted the suggestion. He needed to ferret out who was behind these attacks on Rachel and her son as soon as possible.

"What's wrong?" Rachel asked him.

"Nothing. Just thinking." Tom popped a piece of fish into his mouth.

"Do you know who the first people to see the sunrise every day are?" Jimmy asked, apparently eager to show off a trivia tidbit he'd learned.

"Hmm." Tom scratched his chin pensively. "Well, Japan is called 'the land of the rising sun.' But I think Australia is in an even earlier time zone."

"It's New Zealanders," Jimmy announced. "My teacher told us."

"That's interesting," Tom agreed. "Do you know why the sky turns red at sunset?"

Jimmy leaned forward. "Yup. Light has all kinds of colors in it like the rainbow, and when the sun gets near the water, the waves chop up all the blue light so you only see the red and stuff."

"You're close," Rachel said. "It's because the different colors are different wavelengths, and the short blue ones get scattered by different particles in the atmosphere as the sun nears the horizon."

"Yeah, that's what I meant," Jimmy said.

Rachel's eyes danced with amusement.

"You're a bright boy." Tom offered Jimmy the veggies and dip he'd brought. "I didn't learn that until I was twice your age."

"And I didn't learn it until today," Charlene remarked with a smile.

Jimmy's chest swelled, and Rachel seemed pleased too. She was a good mother. And watching her interact with Charlene, he sensed Rachel cared deeply for her friends too.

After polishing off her clam chowder and fish taco, Charlene got to her feet and stretched. "How would you like to walk on the pier with me, Jimmy?"

"Can I, Mom?" he asked, apparently forgetting their fishing plans.

"Yes," Rachel answered, "but be careful near the water."

"I will." Jimmy dutifully placed his dirty dishes in the designated bag before scampering off with Charlene.

"He's a great kid," Tom said.

"Thank you." Rachel smiled. "I'm rather partial to him."

Her smile did funny things to his heart. He couldn't deny his attraction to her. He didn't want to, if he were honest with himself. He enjoyed spending time with her and her son. "I was thinking—"

"While Charlene has Jimmy out of earshot," she interrupted, "can you fill me in on your conversation with Blake?"

"He claims Richard paid him to keep an eye on your cottage and take care of any necessary maintenance."

"Keep an eye on the cottage?" Rachel echoed. "That's what he said?"

"Yes, and I didn't like how it sounded either."

"Richard told me he hired him to caulk the windows and clean the gutters."

"If Blake had intended to cause any mischief, I'm sure he'll think twice about it now that he knows we're aware of the payoff," Tom reasoned. "I can't definitively link him to the sabotage of your car. Security footage of the store's parking lot didn't show anyone near your car during the time it was parked there. Although we know Blake was in the school parking lot earlier in the day, I haven't found anyone who witnessed him approach your car."

"What about Ellen?"

"She told me she had an appointment off the island. I verified her alibi."

She sighed. "So, we're no closer to putting an end to this."

"I found a torn scrap of fabric where your car had been parked," he said. "Maybe I can match it to a tear in Blake's pants or jacket."

"He'll insist that he tore it working at the school."

"Making a charge stick might not be possible," Tom said. "But hopefully it would dissuade him from trying anything else."

Rachel fiddled with the bandage still covering her burned arm. "Do you think Richard is behind everything that's happened? That he put Blake up to doing it all?"

"The evidence fits," he replied. "Blake could have even told his son to pull some of the pranks at school like the bulletin board and the locked closet. Richard could have easily monkeyed around with the settings on your home's smart system or given Blake the password to do so. And then there's the money. If the work was aboveboard, why did Richard pay Blake in cash? With a receipt he could claim it as an expense of the estate that he seems so eager to wrestle out of your hands."

"Richard was wonderful to Jimmy this week," Rachel said. "I don't want to believe he could do this." She shuddered. "That fire could have killed us."

Tom wrapped an arm around her shoulder. "I'm not going to let anything happen to you and Jimmy. I've requested extra patrols around your house and the school, and I've got a friend watching Blake."

"You do?" Rachel asked, blinking back tears. "I don't know what I would do without your help."

Jimmy dashed up to them. "Can we fish now?" he asked Tom.

Charlene arrived out of breath. "Sorry. I tried to keep him entertained, but he saw a fisherman reel in a huge fish. After that, he was anxious to get back."

"I have a hankering to fish myself." Tom stood. "I'll go grab our gear."

Jimmy tagged along, brimming with fish stories he'd probably heard from the fishermen along the pier.

Tom handed him a rod. "Let's see if we can hook your very own fish story tonight."

Jimmy grinned at him.

Tom chuckled, fondly recalling his own exciting derby fishing exploits with his dad when he was young.

Rachel and Charlene were deep in conversation by the time Tom and Jimmy returned to the beach. They found a spot along the jetty well away from others so that Jimmy could practice his casting without tangling his line with anyone else's.

His third attempt was a keeper, and Rachel and Charlene cheered when he held it up so they could see. Jimmy beamed.

Tom added a lure to his own line. *This is the life.*

Eventually, as the sun began to sink into the ocean, Rachel and Charlene wandered over to them.

"I'm impressed with Jimmy," Charlene commented. "I think I'd tire of the whole exercise pretty quickly if I wasn't getting any nibbles."

"A fisherman has to be patient," Jimmy declared.

Tom nodded. *Truer words have never been spoken, and they don't only apply to fish.* But he couldn't deny that trying to hook Rachel's stalker was testing his patience.

"I'm afraid it's time to stop now," Rachel said to Jimmy. "It'll be past your bedtime when we get home."

"Can't we fish a little longer?" Jimmy begged. "Charlene wants to see the sunset."

"It will be setting in a few minutes," Rachel said. "Please reel in so we can pack up right away afterward."

"Okay," the boy said dejectedly.

"Don't worry, buddy." Tom reeled in his own line so he could assist Jimmy with his. "There will be many more chances to fish."

Jimmy reluctantly reeled in and handed his rod to Tom.

Suddenly, a volley of shots rang out.

15

While cooking pancakes for Saturday's breakfast, Rachel laughed over last night's excitement. Charlene had been in stitches at Tom's reaction to the noisy firecrackers some kid had set off on the beach.

But at the time, Rachel hadn't seen the humor in the situation. Her heart had been in her throat with terror. As soon as the firecrackers had gone off, Tom had dropped the fishing poles and shielded the others with his body. She supposed his reaction had been reflexive. Tom was a police officer, so he was hypersensitive to noises that sounded like gunshots. She smiled. Reflexive or not, his actions had been sweet.

She switched off the stove burner and cocked her head toward the ceiling. Charlene had yet to emerge from her morning shower, and Jimmy was outside picking raspberries to garnish their pancakes.

Rachel glanced out the window to check on his progress and was alarmed to glimpse movement in the side yard. She hurried to the back door. "Jimmy, could you come in now? Breakfast is ready." She stepped onto the deck and craned her neck to see around the side of the house, but no one stepped into view.

Jimmy ran over to her, holding a bowl brimming with raspberries. "I found a ton," he said proudly.

"Great job. I'm sure Charlene will love those on her pancakes." Rachel ushered him inside. "Did you notice anyone outside when you were picking?" she asked as casually as she could manage.

"No. Why?"

"No reason. We'll eat in a few minutes, so go and wash your hands."

Rachel set the platter of pancakes in the middle of the table along with the maple syrup, then rinsed the fresh raspberries. "If a stranger ever came to the house, what should you do?"

Jimmy trotted over to the sink and washed his hands. "Run away from him. Yell for you. Not let him in the house."

"That's right. Very good."

Charlene joined them and busied herself filling three glasses with juice. "What's going on? Did someone show up?"

"No," Rachel said for Jimmy's sake. "I was quizzing Jimmy on how to respond to strangers." She set utensils on the table next to Charlene and whispered into her ear, "I saw movement outside, but it was probably a rabbit or a squirrel."

Charlene nodded without comment, then selected a couple of pancakes and a spoonful of raspberries. "What are our plans for today? A hike in the woods? A walk on the beach?" She grinned at Jimmy. "A trip to the carousel?"

Jimmy's expression crumpled. "Uncle Richard was supposed to take me fishing today."

"Oh." Charlene shuddered. "I suppose we could do that."

Rachel recalled the one and only time they'd fished together as youngsters. Charlene had caught a fairly large fish. When she held it up by the fishing line to have her photo taken, the fish flipped and flopped so much it freed itself from the hook and swatted Charlene in the chest, then landed on her foot. Charlene had screamed as if she were being attacked by a shark. Ever since that day, Charlene had avoided fishing.

Jimmy faced Rachel. "Can we?"

"I'm afraid we don't have any gear," she said.

"We could ask Tom if we can borrow his," Jimmy reasoned.

Rachel chewed on her bottom lip. "Let's plan for another—"

"Speaking of Tom," Charlene interjected. She motioned toward the window. "Here he comes now."

A moment later, Tom knocked on the back door. "I was wondering if Jimmy would like to fish with me at the harbor today."

"Better you than me," Charlene remarked, wrinkling her nose.

"Oh, that's too much to ask of you," Rachel said to Tom.

"Not at all," Tom said. "I'd enjoy the company. And I'm sure you and Charlene would like a chance to catch up without little ears around."

Charlene shot Rachel a smile.

"Can I?" Jimmy asked Rachel. "Please?"

Rachel hesitated. Expecting Tom to watch Jimmy seemed too much to ask of the man on his day off, and there was also Jimmy's safety to think about. What if the person who sabotaged her car went after Jimmy?

As if Charlene could read Rachel's mind, she said, "How could he be any safer than with a police officer?"

Tom nodded but stopped short of pressuring her any further.

Jimmy clasped his hands together and gave her a pleading look. "Please. I promise I'll be good."

Rachel relented. After they finished breakfast, she packed Jimmy a lunch and helped him gather supplies for his adventure.

By the time the pair returned to the kitchen, Tom had armed Charlene with a game plan for a whirlwind tour of some of the highlights of the island Charlene had yet to experience, starting with driving through the dunes on Chappaquiddick Island.

A couple of hours later, immersed in the soothing sights and sounds of ocean waves and migrating birds with her lifelong friend, Rachel sat in the sand and lifted her face to the sun. "I think this might be the first time I've truly relaxed since school started. No, probably longer than that—since my in-laws passed."

"I wish I lived closer to give you a hand," Charlene said.

"You're here now. And I appreciate it. I really needed this."

"I miss our regular girls' night out. Maybe I'll move to the island too. Does Tom have a brother?"

Rachel swatted her arm. "You're terrible."

"You can't still be denying the obvious," Charlene said, rolling her eyes. "Tom invited your son to go fishing for the day. He's clearly smitten."

"He's thoughtful."

"I saw him put his arm around you at the beach."

Rachel frowned. "He didn't."

"He did too," Charlene insisted. "How could you not remember?"

"It must have been when we were talking about Richard. I got upset thinking he could be behind the attacks. Tom was probably just trying to comfort me."

"I'm sorry. I didn't mean to bring that stuff up and get you upset all over again. You deserve a carefree day." Charlene stood. "Shall we go check out the Japanese gardens Tom mentioned?"

"Sure. I haven't been there in years."

They followed the winding paths past rock gardens and through birch groves, then took the footbridge over the pond to the small island in the middle.

Rachel couldn't help but notice that Charlene seemed to grow increasingly anxious.

Charlene peered through the trees across the pond for the third time in as many minutes.

"What's wrong?" Rachel asked.

"I keep getting this eerie feeling someone is watching us."

Rachel stiffened. "Who? Where?"

"That's just it," Charlene said with a huff. "I haven't seen anyone. Not fully anyway. I first sensed someone nearby when we were sitting by the ocean. I glimpsed movement in the trees, but I dismissed it as a fellow hiker. Even here, I'm probably noticing other visitors—all perfectly innocent."

Rachel scanned the garden. "If you're feeling uneasy, then something's not quite right."

Charlene shrugged. "When I checked over my shoulder at the beach, the person immediately ducked behind a tree, as if to step out of sight, then didn't move until after we did. But if he'd been a tourist, he would have simply continued on, especially after he knew I'd spotted him watching us."

"Unless he was too busy watching a bird to even realize you'd seen him," Rachel reasoned. "That could explain why he didn't move afterward."

"I suppose." Charlene didn't sound as if she believed the theory any more than Rachel did. "Why don't we go into town for lunch?"

Rachel agreed. She wouldn't be able to enjoy the garden anymore because she'd be glancing over her shoulder every other minute.

They hurried to their vehicle, but soon after they pulled out of the parking lot, a dark sedan trailed them. Four turns later, the sedan was still there.

"I think we're being followed," Rachel announced.

"I noticed," Charlene said. "Then again, this *is* the road to the ferry, which is the one way off the island with a car."

"Good point," Rachel said, forcing her shoulders to relax. "With any luck, we'll be the last car on the ferry and the guy behind us will have to wait for the next one."

"Or we can hope he makes the same ferry, because then we'd be able to see him for sure," Charlene countered.

Rachel slowed. "Peek out the back window, and see if you can make out the license plate number."

Charlene released her seat belt and climbed into the back seat. "He slowed too. Oh no. Another car passed him."

"I could park off to the side at the ferry, and we could watch for him," Rachel suggested. "There should be lots of people around, so I'm not too worried he'd try anything."

"I'm game if you are."

Rachel backed into a parking spot shielded by a larger truck. "Can you see him coming?"

They both angled left and right to peer out different windows, but the truck hiding them from view also made it difficult to see what was coming.

"There he is," Charlene said as a sedan passed.

"Are you sure?" Rachel squinted at the license plate, but she could read only one number. She jumped out of the SUV for a better angle.

The car drove straight onto the ferry—the last vehicle that would fit—and the gate was immediately closed.

Rachel hurried toward the water with Charlene close behind her. "I can't make out the license plate. Can you?"

"No, the rail is in the way."

Rachel climbed onto a cement abutment, but the ferry had already started across the water. She reached into her pocket for her phone, but it wasn't there. "Give me your phone. I'll take a picture, and maybe we can zoom in enough to see the number."

Charlene tapped the screen to bring up the camera app, then handed her phone over.

Rachel focused on the last car and snapped the photo. After she returned the phone to Charlene, she hopped down. "Can you see the license plate number?"

Charlene zoomed in on the image. "No, the rail is still blocking the view. Perhaps if we download the picture to your computer, we can spot some other identifiable feature on the car or at least the make and model."

"Do you think we could be mistaken about him following us?"

"I don't know. Your stories might have me a little keyed up."

"I guess we'll know if he's waiting for us after we cross."

Charlene shivered. "This kind of thing seems a lot more adventurous when you read about it in a novel."

"Having fun?" Tom asked Jimmy. The boy hadn't caught anything yet, but he seemed as eager as when they'd started more than two hours earlier.

Jimmy beamed. "Yeah, this is great!"

Tom set down his fishing rod and fired up the engine on his small motorboat. This was usually a good spot to fish for false albacore and bonitos, but nothing was biting this morning. "I'll putter the boat around to see if we can't chase up some fish."

Jimmy squealed as a spray of salt water caught him in the face.

"Hang on," Tom said.

Jimmy's life jacket was hiked comically up to his ears, and his little arms stretched from one side of the boat to the other. He couldn't quite reach both gunnels and settled for holding on to the edge of his seat. "There's some!" He pointed to a boil, then frantically attempted to cast his lure into the fray.

The hook caught Tom's ear, sending a wave of pain throughout his body. He stopped the boat.

Jimmy spun around, and the color drained from his cheeks, leaving them whiter than the underbelly of an albacore. "I'm sorry." He moved toward Tom as if to help, but the motion jiggled the boat and his fishing rod, causing a painful tug on the hook piercing Tom's ear.

"It's okay. Stay still." Tom clicked open his pocketknife and sliced the line before Jimmy inadvertently caused more damage. Gritting his teeth, Tom attempted to remove the hook from the edge of his ear.

"Does it hurt?" Jimmy asked, his voice quavering.

Tom grimaced. "A little." His attempts to remove the hook were useless, thanks to the barb that was meant to keep a hooked fish from escaping.

Tears trickled down Jimmy's cheeks.

"Hey, it's not as bad as all that. We'll go back to the dock, and I'm sure someone will be able to snip the barb so the hook can slide right out." Tom stifled a cringe at the thought of where the hook had been before it pierced his ear. He'd have to cleanse his ear with antiseptic.

Jimmy burst into tears. His shoulders heaved, and his sobs came quicker. "You're bleeding."

Tom glanced at his hand, surprised an ear would produce so much blood. He gingerly pressed a tissue at the torn flesh. "I promise this is no big deal. These kinds of things happen to fishermen all the time. This is one of those stories you'll tell your friends for years to come."

Jimmy shook his head. "You won't tell Mom, will you? She'll never let me fish again."

Tom laughed. "Of course she will. From Charlene's expression when I suggested taking you fishing, I suspect they have a similar fishing story of their own."

Jimmy widened his eyes. "Really?"

"Really." Tom revved the motor and steered the boat toward shore.

By the time Tom moored the boat, Jimmy had calmed down. But after scanning the dock, Tom realized he wasn't going to find any help. He assisted Jimmy out of the boat and removed the boy's life jacket. "Well, I think we might have to go to the hospital and have a doctor snip this hook out. I'll give your mom a call to let her know what's going on."

Jimmy burst into tears once more.

"It's okay," Tom soothed. "You don't want your mom to hear you crying and think something is wrong, do you?"

Jimmy sniffled.

Rachel answered on the first ring. "Is everything all right? Did something happen to Jimmy?"

Tom was surprised by how worried she sounded. "No, he's fine. We're both fine. Are you and Charlene having a good time?" He held the phone a little too close to the hook in his ear and winced, then moved the phone to his other ear.

"We are," she said. "For a while we thought someone might be following us, but now we're not so sure, since there is only one main road across Chappaquiddick."

Now Rachel's reaction made sense. Tom took Jimmy's hand and started toward the truck as he talked. "But you're both okay?"

"Yes. We're having lunch now."

"Did you get the car's license plate number?"

"Unfortunately, no, not even a make and model. But I'm sure it was an older model sedan because it didn't have daytime running lights. And it was dark blue."

"Dark gray," Charlene corrected in the background.

"Do you think so?" Rachel asked Charlene. The question was followed by a muffled dispute on their end of the phone.

"I called to let you know we had a bit of a mishap with a fishhook," Tom interjected, "and we're heading to the hospital to have it removed."

"What?" Rachel yelped.

Jimmy started crying again. More like bawling.

"It's no big deal," Tom told Rachel. "I can't get the hook out myself because of the barb."

A kerfuffle sounded over the phone. "We're on our way. We'll meet you there." Rachel hung up.

"That went well," Tom said sardonically. He rested a hand on Jimmy's shoulder. "Come on. Dry your eyes. We don't want your mom to worry when she sees you."

Ellen waved to them as they reached his truck. To his surprise, given their last encounter, she closed the distance between them. "How was the fishing today?"

"Jimmy caught a big one," Tom joked and turned his head to show off his new fishhook earring.

Ellen flipped up the large brim on her sun hat and gasped.

Tom regarded his ear in his pickup's side mirror. It did look a little gruesome. "We're headed to the ER to get it removed."

"Where's Jimmy's mother?" she asked, straightening her pink top.

"She's meeting us there."

"But you can't drive like that," Ellen said. "I'll take you."

Tom shook his head. "It's all right. I can handle it."

"I won't take no for an answer," she insisted. "What would happen if you suddenly passed out from blood loss or something?"

Jimmy's bottom lip began to quiver.

Tom squeezed his shoulder reassuringly, although he had to admit, he was feeling a little light-headed. "If you insist," Tom agreed. "I suppose it might be safer."

"When we get there, I'll take care of Jimmy until his mom arrives," Ellen offered. "He'll be safe with me."

Tom glanced sidelong at her, wondering why she'd felt the need to clarify that. Would Jimmy really be safe with her? But what choice did he have?

16

Rachel scarcely stopped at the next stop sign before hitting the gas again. "I knew I shouldn't have let Jimmy go fishing."

"What did Tom say happened?" Charlene asked.

"They have to go to the hospital."

"You already told me that. But why?"

"I don't know exactly. Something about a fishhook. Jimmy sounded inconsolable." Rachel's chest constricted. "I should have been with him."

"I'm sorry." Charlene grabbed the dash as Rachel took the curve a little too quickly. "I know you let him go for my sake."

"Please don't think I'm blaming you," Rachel said. "I can't get the image out of my mind of how shaken Jimmy was the day someone said those awful things to him over the phone. I promised I'd never leave him alone like that again."

"You can't be with him every second of the day. And you didn't leave him alone. He was with a policeman you know personally."

Rachel veered into the hospital parking lot and scanned the vehicles. "I don't see Tom's truck. He was closer to the hospital than us. He should be here by now."

Ellen walked out the ER door. She held the hand of a wailing young boy.

"That's Jimmy!" Rachel swerved into a parking spot, jumped out of the SUV, and sprinted over to them. "What are you doing with my son?" She snatched Jimmy from the woman's clutches, then dropped to her knees and folded him into her arms.

Jimmy buried his face in Rachel's shoulder, his tears dampening her shirt.

Ellen stepped back. "I was at the harbor when Tom docked. When I saw how pale he was, I offered to drive him to the hospital and watch Jimmy while the doctor examined Tom's injury."

Charlene joined them. "Tom's the one who got hurt? Not Jimmy?" She shot Rachel a look.

Rachel wasn't sure how to interpret it, so she ignored it. "It's okay." She gently nudged Jimmy from her arms enough to wipe his tears. "I thought you were hurt. Why are you so upset?"

"Tom has a barbed fishhook caught in his ear," Ellen explained. "The sight made me a tad squeamish. I can see how it would have been upsetting for Jimmy."

"It's my fault!" Jimmy wailed.

"I told your son this kind of thing can happen to anyone," Ellen said soothingly. "I'd hoped walking outside while we waited would help him calm down."

Rachel got to her feet, still holding Jimmy close, her gaze fixed on the woman. She knew she should thank Ellen, but Rachel wasn't sure she believed the woman's intentions were honorable.

Charlene extended her hand to Ellen and thanked her for taking care of Jimmy. "We'll drive Tom back to the dock to retrieve his truck after he's finished here."

"Are you sure?" Ellen asked. "If you want to take Jimmy home, that's perfectly understandable. I don't mind waiting to give Tom a lift."

"That's all right," Rachel said, her tone clipped.

Ellen raised her chin. "I guess I'll see you around." She shifted her gaze to Jimmy, and her expression softened. "Take care, and please don't feel bad." She strode away.

"She seems like a nice woman," Charlene remarked. "Why were you so terse with her?"

"That was Ellen Donovan, the substitute teacher from my school," Rachel answered. "Remember I told you about her?" She punctuated her explanation with a telling glance toward Jimmy.

"Oh, *her*." Charlene nodded. "Now I get it."

Rachel placed her hand on Jimmy's shoulder. "We'd better go in to see how Tom is coming along."

Jimmy dragged his feet as they started toward the ER doors.

"Come on," Rachel urged. "Don't you want to see how Tom's doing?"

Jimmy shook his head vehemently. "He's going to hate me."

"No, he won't," Charlene assured him. "It was an accident."

The ER doors glided open, and they stepped inside.

Tom emerged from another set of doors, and he grinned when he noticed them. "I'm as good as new." He dangled a barbed fishhook in the air. "Should we frame this so you can tell the story of your first big catch?"

Jimmy shrank behind Rachel and shook his head.

"What were you thinking, leaving Jimmy in Ellen's care?" Rachel hissed.

"What happened?" Tom asked. He cocked his head and made eye contact with Jimmy. "Did Miss Donovan make you feel uncomfortable?"

Jimmy shook his head again.

Rachel frowned. "That's not the point."

"If you're still upset about hooking my ear, don't be," Tom said to Jimmy. "Honestly, I'm looking forward to having a fun fishing derby story to tell the guys at work."

Jimmy edged out from behind Rachel's legs. "Really?"

"Yes, really," Tom said.

"The story might have ended differently if we hadn't gotten here when we did," Rachel muttered under her breath. But she refrained from demanding any more answers since her anger was clearly adding to Jimmy's distress.

Tom scratched his chin, watching Rachel march out of the ER with Jimmy. He hadn't expected such vitriol from her over a minor mishap. Maybe her earlier scare with Charlene, where they thought they were being followed, had rattled Rachel more than she'd let on over the phone.

Charlene touched his arm as he started to follow them. "We told Ellen we'd give you a lift to pick up your truck. You feel okay to drive home from there?"

"I'm fine," he said. "It wasn't that big of a deal."

Ahead of them, Rachel harrumphed.

"Don't take her reaction personally," Charlene whispered. "Rachel's been leery of Ellen since you admitted your suspicions about her. Ellen was walking out of the hospital with Jimmy when we arrived, so naturally Rachel's first thought was that Ellen was kidnapping him."

Tom wanted to kick himself. "No wonder Rachel's so upset."

As Rachel helped Jimmy buckle into his seat, Charlene urged Tom to sit in the front passenger seat so he could enjoy more legroom.

Rachel closed Jimmy's door and addressed Tom. "I'm sorry for overreacting. And I feel horrible over how much pain you suffered, even though you put on a brave face for Jimmy's sake. I totally understand why you needed to accept a ride with Ellen. Please forgive me."

Tom offered her a warm smile. "There's nothing to forgive. I probably would have been fine driving myself, but I figured it's better safe than sorry."

Rachel gave him a sheepish expression. "Does your ear still hurt?"

"No, the only thing that hurts is my arm where they had to give me a tetanus shot," he answered.

"I'm sorry about what happened," Rachel said.

"I have to admit it was stressful," Tom said. "I realized I couldn't get the hook out myself at the same time I was trying to console Jimmy and convince him there was nothing to worry about."

"Thank you for taking such good care of him," she said. "As you can see, Jimmy inherited a tendency to overreact from me."

He laughed.

"I appreciate how sweet you were about the whole ordeal—more concerned about Jimmy than yourself—especially after the reception I gave you back there."

"Don't sweat it," Tom said. "I told you to sign up Jimmy for the derby, didn't I?"

"Yes, but what do you mean?" Rachel asked, sounding confused.

"I doubt any of the other kids will score a bigger catch than me," he joked.

Her cheeks grew pink, making her prettier than ever. "I feel bad all this kept you from an entire day of derby fishing."

"I don't care about the competition," Tom said. "I thoroughly enjoyed fishing with Jimmy this morning."

"Guys!" Charlene shouted from the other side of the vehicle.

"What?" Rachel asked.

Tom gazed over the hood and noticed Charlene's grimace. On high alert, he shifted to shield Rachel and scanned the vicinity. "What is it?" he hissed at Charlene, who still hadn't answered.

"Richard's SUV." Charlene gestured to the driver's side door. "Someone keyed it."

17

Rachel scowled at the vandalized SUV door. "I don't believe this. Richard's going to kill me."

Tom ran his finger along the scarred paint. "Is this the first you noticed the damage?"

"Yes," Rachel answered. "If someone did it earlier in the day, I'm sure I would have seen it as soon as I opened the door."

"What possesses people to do things like this?" Charlene walked around the neighboring parked cars, checking their doors. "No one else's car was targeted. Do you think the guy who was following us did it?"

"No, I think it was Ellen," Rachel said.

"I find that hard to believe," Charlene said. "You weren't the friendliest toward her, but she had to know you'd suspect her because you saw her here."

"Maybe, but like you said, my vehicle was the only one targeted," Rachel said. "And Ellen saw me pull in. No one else knew I was driving the Range Rover."

"The guy who tailed us to the ferry knew too," Charlene reminded her.

Tom frowned, but he didn't voice his opinion.

"I'm hungry," Jimmy called from inside the vehicle.

"I'm afraid your lunch is at the harbor in my truck," Tom told him, then addressed the two women. "The poor kid hasn't eaten since we had a snack around ten."

Charlene slid into the back seat beside Jimmy. "Sorry we took so long out there, kiddo. We'll get you some lunch now."

Tom got into the passenger seat. "I'll come back later and ask security if they have any video surveillance on the parking lot. I can talk to Ellen, but I doubt she'll fess up unless I have proof."

Rachel didn't say anything as she climbed behind the steering wheel. She drove to the harbor in silence, doing her best to tamp down her anger over the keying. One thing was for certain—Richard wasn't behind this. Even if he'd paid Blake to follow her, Blake wouldn't be foolish enough to vandalize Richard's own vehicle.

Rachel parked next to Tom's pickup.

"Do you want to keep fishing while you eat lunch?" Tom asked Jimmy.

"No!" Rachel exclaimed, then got her tone under control. "No," she repeated. "I think he's had enough excitement for one day."

"These kinds of mishaps are like falling off a horse," Tom responded. "He needs to get back on as soon as possible. We don't want him to be afraid of casting his line next time he goes fishing."

"You're right," Rachel conceded. "But perhaps we could plan on another day. Jimmy seems exhausted." She grabbed Jimmy's backpack from Tom's truck.

"I'm going to stick around and fish some more," Tom said. "I'll let you know if I learn anything from hospital security."

Rachel thanked him, and they said their goodbyes. Then Rachel, Charlene, and Jimmy left Tom on his own to try to catch the big one.

"Are you okay?" Charlene asked quietly as they exited the parking lot and headed to Rachel's house.

"I'm sorry," Rachel said. "This isn't much of a holiday for you, with me stewing over cars that may or may not be following us, impromptu hospital visits, and vehicle damage."

"I came here to be supportive," Charlene reminded her. "I wish

Tom had suggested checking out those hospital security tapes while we were still there. I'll bet our vandal was the same guy we spotted trailing us."

"If it's not Ellen, we can ask Tom to arrange for us to watch the security footage."

Charlene laughed.

"What's so funny?"

"I was remembering how you blew up at him when you found him in the hospital. The poor guy didn't know what hit him."

Sighing, Rachel slouched in her seat. "I feel terrible about that." She glanced in the rearview mirror. Jimmy had already fallen asleep. "Tom probably regrets the day I moved here. I'm sure he must think I'm nothing but a magnet for trouble."

"Oh, trust me," Charlene said with a smile. "That's *not* what he thinks."

Rachel rolled her eyes. "He's taking care of a citizen in distress like a good cop should."

Charlene burst out laughing. "You are seriously deluded."

Fortunately, Rachel parked at the cottage and escaped the SUV before her friend could expound on her total misconception of the way things were between her and Tom. Planning to carry their stuff into the house before waking Jimmy, Rachel grabbed his backpack and the other supplies she'd packed and walked to the cottage. Her arms were so full that she had to feel her way up the porch steps with her foot. Her shoe squashed something soft.

Reflexively, Rachel jerked backward and dropped the stuff she'd been carrying on the ground.

A dead mouse adorned her porch.

"Your neighborhood cat left you a present," Charlene remarked as she came up beside her.

Rachel stifled a shudder and stomped to the garden shed for a shovel. "There are no cats around here." She scooped up the poor creature and deposited it under a bush at the edge of the property. "Except for Tom, all the neighbors are away for the winter." Turning back to Charlene, Rachel gripped the shovel tighter and swallowed hard. "This was the handiwork of my stalker."

Charlene squinted at the smudge on the porch, her face ashen.

Rachel sighed. "If the sight of the aftermath is bothering you that much, I'd better take the hose to the porch before I wake up Jimmy."

"No, someone left you a message."

Tom removed his fishing gear from his truck parked at the harbor, then decided not to resume fishing. He couldn't stop thinking about Rachel. She'd tried to mask her fear with anger, but the signs were unmistakable—her dilated pupils, trembling hands, and the scrambled way she recounted their encounter with Ellen and the guy they'd earlier believed was following them.

He wished the Japanese gardens had security footage he could analyze to determine if Charlene had been right about the man following them. After everything that had happened to Rachel lately, he wouldn't be surprised if their imaginations had simply gotten the best of them. But he didn't want to take anything for granted.

After loading his gear back into his truck, he returned to the hospital and went to the security office. He explained his suspicions about the vehicle damage to the guard on duty. They reviewed the security footage for the time in question.

Three different people passed within keying distance of the Range

Rover—a male of average height, a woman with long hair, and a woman in a sun hat of the same style Ellen had been wearing.

"Can you replay that part one more time?" Tom asked the security guard.

The man nodded and pressed a few buttons.

Tom scrutinized the woman in the hat more closely. The video showed only a rear view. At the time, he'd been distracted by the hook in his ear, so he hadn't paid close attention to what Ellen had been wearing. He remembered her sun hat and her pink top. Unfortunately, the footage was in black-and-white. However, the woman's gait reminded him of Ellen's. And the woman slowed her pace by the driver's side door of the Range Rover and glanced around, as if to make sure no one was watching.

Tom recorded the section of video on his phone. After thanking the security guard, Tom left the hospital and drove to Ellen's house. He could see Ellen keying the vehicle out of spite for Rachel's hostile reception. But a question kept nagging him: Would Ellen have left the grounds with Jimmy if Rachel hadn't arrived when she did?

Either way, he'd clearly been too quick to scratch Ellen off his suspect list.

He exited the truck and walked to the front door.

Ellen cheerfully welcomed Tom inside her home for a glass of iced tea. "How are you feeling?" she asked as they sat down in her living room. "Your ear looks a lot better."

"Yeah, it doesn't hurt at all. I appreciate your help getting to the hospital."

Her cheeks flushed. "You didn't have to come all the way over here to thank me for that. I was happy to do it."

He paused. "Actually, that's not why I came by."

"Oh?" Wariness replaced her cheerful demeanor.

"When we left the hospital, we noticed the door of Rachel's SUV had been vandalized," Tom said. "Someone dragged a key through the paint."

Ellen's face reddened, and her eyes blazed. "You think I did it?" Her voice pitched higher. "After I went out of my way to help you?"

"The security footage shows you pausing near the driver's door," he said, even though he wasn't positive Ellen was the woman in the video.

Ellen slammed down her glass and surged to her feet. "I can't believe this is how you and Rachel show your thanks." She stalked to the window, then spun on her heel and glared at him. "She acted like a crazy woman when she saw me with Jimmy. Did she tell you that?"

"Someone has been harassing Rachel and Jimmy," Tom said. "She'd naturally feel defensive seeing someone she didn't expect leading her son from the hospital, especially given how distressed he was."

"I didn't do any of those other things."

Tom took a sip of his iced tea. He'd confirmed her alibi for the day of the car fire. But that didn't mean she wasn't behind any of the incidents. She could have an accomplice.

As if his silence unnerved her, she blurted, "What motive could I possibly have? I hardly know the woman. In fact, I don't think many people on this island know her. Has it occurred to you that her saboteur followed her here from Boston?"

"Yes, but several of the incidents occurred at the school, which has monitored access, as you know."

"Several?" Ellen repeated. "Are you sure she's not simply getting melodramatic over some schoolboy pranks?" She shook her head. "I've fallen for some doozies as a substitute teacher."

"Perhaps," he said. If Ellen hoped to convince the principal that Rachel wasn't equipped for the job, creating the perception that Rachel was overreacting to schoolboy pranks would suit her agenda.

And instigating a few insidious situations outside the school to make Rachel all the more wary would add to the paranoid personality Ellen could have hoped to spark. "Do you deny keying the car?"

She crossed her arms over her chest. "I'm deeply offended that you even feel the need to ask."

"Is that a yes?"

"Wasn't it obvious? And now, if there's nothing else..."

"I'm sorry for bothering you." Tom got up and strode to the front door. "Thank you again for your help earlier. I appreciate it."

Ellen nodded as she opened the door for him. She closed it before he reached his truck.

When he slid behind the wheel, a text message alert sounded from Rachel: *Please come to my place as soon as you can.*

Tom's pulse spiked. He couldn't believe something else had happened. How much more could Rachel handle? *Be there in ten minutes.*

He stepped on the gas and made it in seven.

Rachel sprang out the front door the instant he swerved into the driveway. Charlene stood inside at the picture window, watching. Rachel met him halfway up the walk.

"What happened?" Tom asked.

"Someone left a dead mouse on the front porch." Rachel led him to the spot. "And a message."

Tom's breath caught, burning his lungs. Smeared in bloodred letters, the message declared: *I know where you live.*

18

Tired of tossing and turning all night, Rachel crawled out of bed at five o'clock Sunday morning and put on the coffeepot. Then she checked the locks on all the windows and doors, even though Tom had done it the night before. At least having Charlene here for the weekend had kept her from becoming a total basket case.

The aroma of brewing coffee drew her back to the kitchen. Rachel decided to make waffles for breakfast. She couldn't let Jimmy see her so discombobulated. She dug a bag of frozen blueberries out of the freezer to make his favorite topping to go with them.

Charlene entered the kitchen and yawned. "I thought I smelled coffee."

"Sorry. Did I wake you?"

"Don't worry about it. At least *I* got some sleep. By the looks of it, that's more than you can say."

Rachel poured a large mug of coffee. "If you keep it up, I won't make you waffles with blueberry topping."

"I've got a better idea." Charlene pried the mug from Rachel's hand. "Get into your sweats and go for a run. I'll stay here with Jimmy."

"But—"

Charlene raised a hand, cutting her off. "You said you missed running. You know it'll energize you and help clear your head."

Rachel grimaced. "I'm not sure I feel safe running my secluded road alone after yesterday's 'gift' on my front porch."

With a grin, Charlene raised a finger. "I already thought of that. Your bodyguard will be here in five minutes."

"My bodyguard?" Rachel gasped. "You didn't."

"Ask Tom?" Charlene said innocently, then sipped the coffee she'd commandeered from Rachel. "Of course I did. He's going for a run anyway. Why not run with you?"

"I'll slow him down."

Charlene spurted coffee in her sudden burst of laughter. "You were our school's cross-country champion. I'm sure you can hold your own."

"That was a long time ago," Rachel reminded her.

"You're still in great shape." Charlene set the coffee mug down and clapped. "Come on. You don't want to keep the man waiting."

Rachel hurried to her bedroom and put on a pair of yoga pants, a T-shirt, and a sweatshirt. Studying herself in the mirror, she cringed. She usually didn't wear makeup, but she needed some today.

She applied a little concealer to tone down the bags under her eyes and touched up her lashes with waterproof mascara. Fixing her hair proved to be a hopeless endeavor, so she grabbed an elastic and pulled what hair she could into a high ponytail, then used a headband to tame the rest.

After grabbing her running shoes from the closet, Rachel hurried back to the kitchen. "Okay, I'm as ready as I'll ever be, though I'm still a mess."

"Hardly," Tom replied.

His deep voice made her heart miss a beat. "Oh," Rachel squeaked. She swallowed hard. "I didn't realize you were already here." She dropped into the closest chair to put on her shoes.

"I'm early," he said. "I was excited to have a running partner for a change."

Rachel glanced at him, and her heart fluttered at the genuine look of pleasure on his face. She quickly tied her shoes and stood. "I haven't warmed up, so perhaps we can start out slow."

Tom grinned. "You've got it."

"Don't worry about breakfast," Charlene said, waving them off. "I'll take care of the waffles."

"Thanks," Rachel said. "We'll be back soon."

They started at a comfortable jog in companionable silence.

A few hundred yards in, Tom asked, "Did you get any sleep last night?"

She snorted. "No."

"Me either."

"Because of me?" The news surprised Rachel and made her feel oddly comforted at the same time.

He nodded. "I hope it doesn't worry you more to know that I'm concerned for you too."

"Now that you put it that way and knowing you're a cop, I guess it should."

"I was thinking we should install security cameras separate from the smart system that don't use Wi-Fi—something I should've suggested from day one."

"Good idea," Rachel said. "Although I won't hold my breath that it will be much of a deterrent."

"No, maybe not," Tom admitted. "But if he comes back, the cameras might help us to ID him."

"You're right. It will feel good to do something proactive instead of waiting and wondering when the next attack will come."

"I'm sorry I haven't been able to figure out who's been harassing you," he said quietly. "Or get any proof against those we suspect."

"I know you're doing more than any other officer would," she responded. "And I appreciate all your efforts."

Tom sped up, his jaw clenched.

Suspecting his pent-up emotions were fueling him, she said, "Don't beat yourself up over this. I know you're doing all you can."

"It's not enough. I should have located this guy by now. What's the use of being a cop if I can't keep horrible people from harassing—" He abruptly stopped. "I'm sorry. This run was supposed to help you work off stress, not add to it."

Rachel smiled. "To be honest, it makes me feel better knowing I'm not the only one this guy is driving crazy."

Tom chuckled. "Let's not allow him to ruin the rest of our morning run."

They continued in silence, enjoying the birdsong and the rising sun as it peeked through the trees. Houses along the gravel road were few and far between, and they appeared to be vacant. The observation made Rachel realize how safe she felt with Tom. If she'd ventured out for a run like this alone, she would have been jumping at shadows while every disturbing event of late replayed in an endless loop through her thoughts.

"I'm glad Charlene suggested this," Rachel said as they neared home and slowed their pace to cool down.

"Perhaps we can do it again sometime," Tom suggested. "Jimmy could ride his bike with us."

"Yes, that would be fun." As her front porch came into view, she determinedly shut down the memory of the mouse. She didn't want to spoil the last day of Charlene's visit with useless worry.

Tom bypassed the front of the house and jogged beside her to the back door next to the kitchen.

Charlene poked her head out, fork in hand. "Would you like to join us for waffles?" she asked Tom. "I made plenty."

"Thanks for the offer, but I can't today. I'm on ushering duty at church this morning, and I still need to shower." He touched Rachel's arm. "Don't hesitate to call if you notice anything or anyone that concerns you."

"I won't," Rachel said. "Thank you."

Charlene grinned when Rachel entered the kitchen. "Enjoy your run?"

The teasing in her voice prompted Rachel to toss a nearby dish towel at her friend. "You're terrible. But yes, I did. Thank you for arranging it and watching Jimmy."

"He's still in bed. You might as well go wake him. The waffles are done. I just need to whip the cream."

"He's still in bed?" Rachel asked. She checked the clock on the wall. "He never sleeps this late." She raced out of the kitchen and up the stairs two at a time.

Where was her son?

As Tom was leaving, he glimpsed Rachel through the front window and watched her race upstairs. Something was wrong. He ran to the back door. Thankfully, she'd forgotten to lock it, so he let himself in.

The kitchen was empty. He entered the living room in time to spot Charlene rounding the top of the stairs. He followed her.

By the time he reached the upstairs hallway, both women stood outside Jimmy's bedroom. Rachel clutched her chest, her face pale.

Jimmy.

"What's wrong?" Tom blurted.

Rachel shook her head. "Nothing. Jimmy's fine. Charlene thought he wasn't awake yet. He never sleeps this late, so I assumed the worst." Her words tumbled over each other. "But he was playing with his toys in his room. I overreacted again."

His heart ached for her. "That's only natural." He paused, thinking, then said, "I'd like to drive you to and from school this week. I have evening shifts at work, so it won't be a problem, and I'll feel better knowing you're safe on the drive at least."

He expected her to argue, but instead she mused, "It would also give me a chance to take Richard's SUV to a body shop to get the damage repaired from the keying. Are you sure it's not an imposition?"

"Not at all," he assured her.

"Thank you," she said softly. "I don't know what we'd do without you. I feel like everything is falling apart."

"Why don't you take a nice shower?" Charlene suggested, putting an arm around Rachel's shoulders. "It'll give you a chance to calm down."

Rachel nodded and headed for the bathroom.

"After she has a hot shower and gets some food in her, she'll be all right," Charlene told him. "I'll make sure of it."

With a heavy sigh, Tom thanked Charlene and started home once more. This time, he didn't feel nearly as optimistic as he had been mere minutes ago.

Tom needed to arrest the lowlife who was tormenting Rachel. Clearly, his psychological tactics were starting to take a toll on her.

After breakfast, Rachel, Charlene, and Jimmy decided to go to church. Tom greeted them at the door and ushered them to their seats. Rachel tried not to notice how handsome he was in his suit. When the service was over, Tom introduced them to his mother. The four of them chatted while Katy and Jimmy visited the refreshments table.

By the time they left church, it was nearly lunchtime, so Rachel took Charlene and Jimmy to the beach for a picnic.

As soon as Jimmy finished eating, he grabbed his sand pail and set off in search of conch shells.

Reclining on her elbows on the beach blanket, Charlene grinned at his enthusiasm over his finds. "Jimmy is so sweet. You're really blessed to have such a wonderful son."

"Yes, I certainly am," Rachel agreed. "With everything that's been going on, I need to count my blessings more often. I'm lucky that I have a good job and live in such an amazing place."

"You're also lucky to live near such a great guy. He clearly likes you a lot."

Rachel's cheeks heated.

Charlene laughed. "Admit it. You like him too."

"He's very nice."

"And fabulous with Jimmy," Charlene added.

"He doesn't deserve to get involved with a jinx," Rachel said.

Charlene cocked her head. "What are you talking about?"

"We've already had this conversation. I'm a jinx. Everyone I love dies." Rachel bit her lip, her gaze straying to her son. "I live in fear that Jimmy will be next."

"You're *not* a jinx," Charlene insisted. "I'm your best friend, and I haven't been struck by lightning yet."

Rachel squirmed, uncomfortable with the direction of the conversation. "Can we talk about something else?"

Charlene sprang to her feet. "Let's walk the beach."

They spent the rest of the afternoon enjoying the sunshine, each other's company, and the beautiful ocean vistas, talking about nothing in particular.

But that evening as Rachel and Jimmy waited with Charlene for her ferry to board, Charlene became serious. "Please promise me that you'll at least be open to letting a little romance into your life."

Rachel gulped and shot a glance in Jimmy's direction, but mercifully, he seemed oblivious to the conversation.

Boarding for the ferry began, and Charlene nudged Rachel's arm. "Promise?"

"I promise to think about it."

Charlene's victorious grin made Rachel's heart do a funny hiccup. What had she just agreed to? Was she really ready for that?

19

"These aren't my tests," Rachel told the school secretary Monday morning. She slid the file folder across the desk.

"I photocopied them from the master you left in your file." The woman thumbed through the stack of papers in the folder and removed the last page with a yellow memo attached. "It says, 'Please make 25 copies for Monday. Thanks, Rachel Sound.'"

"Well, that's my note, but this isn't the test I attached it to. This is primary school material. Perhaps the grade two or three teacher picked up my papers by mistake?"

The secretary gave the folder back to Rachel. "You can ask Mr. Nichols. He picked up a folder for his class this morning."

"Thanks." Rachel checked her watch and rushed out. If Ed Nichols didn't have her papers, she would have barely enough time to print a new master and make copies for herself. She should have done that in the first place.

Rachel hurried down the hall and found Ed printing a spelling list on the whiteboard in his otherwise empty classroom. "I was wondering if you received my class tests by mistake."

"I don't think so." He went to his desk and opened a folder similar to the one she'd been given. "Sorry, but these are the tests I requested."

Rachel showed him the contents of her folder. "I received the same."

"Maybe the secretary forgot to switch the master when she made your copies." Ed reached for Rachel's folder. "I can hang on to those."

"Of course." Rachel rushed to her classroom to grab her backup USB drive from her purse, then returned to the office.

The secretary was no longer there, so Rachel went ahead and borrowed her computer to print the test master and took it to the copier.

Principal Sutton stepped out of his office next door and made a show of checking the time. "Cutting it close, aren't you?"

"Yes," she agreed. "The secretary accidentally gave me photocopies of another class's tests."

"In the future, it's probably best if you take care of your own copying."

Rachel cringed at the censure in his voice. "Yes sir."

The photocopier beeped an error message three copies shy of the number she required.

Rachel stifled a groan. "The display says the machine is out of toner. You wouldn't happen to know where that's stored, would you, sir?"

Jack strode in with a case of copier paper and a smaller box on top. "I have the toner here. The secretary asked me to fetch a new cartridge for her."

"You're a lifesaver," Rachel said.

The custodian chuckled. "I don't hear that much. Happy to help." He installed the new cartridge in a flash.

Rachel finished the last of her copies, then grabbed the stack and her master. "Have a good day, gentlemen."

When the office door closed behind her, she faintly heard Jack say, "I've noticed that new teacher seems a bit disorganized. Always seems to be losing things."

Rachel slowed, but the principal replied too quietly for her to make out his response. She sighed. This wasn't the impression she'd wanted to make on her boss in her first month on the job.

The next morning, Rachel escorted her class to the school library. The librarian stopped her at the door. "I'm sorry. You need to schedule a time for your class, so we have only one group in at a time."

"I *did* schedule my class," Rachel said. "For nine o'clock this morning."

Shaking her head, the librarian strode to her computer.

Rachel instructed her class to stand quietly in line at the door and followed the woman to her desk. A middle grade class occupied the central tables and was being instructed in library research skills.

The librarian opened the schedule and pointed to the screen. "Mrs. Dixon's class is scheduled. She booked the time slot yesterday."

"I booked the slot last week," Rachel said. "Someone erased my booking."

"Are you sure you don't have the wrong day?" The librarian scrolled through the schedules. "There you are. You have next Tuesday at nine."

"I know I didn't book that day," Rachel insisted.

The librarian shrugged, clearly thinking that Rachel was mistaken, if not delusional.

Rachel straightened. First mixed-up test papers, now this. They couldn't both be accidents. Her prankster was still messing with her. But was it the same person who'd left the dead mouse on her porch?

"Did you hear me?" the librarian asked.

"I'm sorry," Rachel said, snapping out of her reverie. "What was that?"

"As you can see, I can't accommodate you at the moment. If you'd like to bring your class back at eleven, I could fit you in then."

"Yes, that would work," Rachel said. "Thank you."

When Rachel rejoined her class outside the library, Mr. Sutton was chatting to her students. "Problem, Mrs. Sound?"

"Just a scheduling glitch," Rachel answered, resisting the urge to cast blame. "Class, we'll return to our room now."

Grumbling, the students headed toward the classroom.

"Are you having trouble getting used to our systems here?" the principal asked Rachel.

"No sir. I seem to have a prankster determined to foil my plans."

"A prankster?" Mr. Sutton repeated. "If that's the case, we must nip it in the bud. Do you suspect a particular student?"

"No." She bit her tongue. She could hardly cast aspersions on Ellen without any proof.

"Well, when you do, send him straight to me, and I'll speak to him."

"Thank you, sir. I'll do that." By the time Rachel reached her classroom, the students' chatter was loud enough to be heard in the hall. "Please quiet down, and take out your math textbooks."

For the remainder of the day, she struggled to keep her frustration at bay.

After school, Katy took Jimmy outside to jump rope on the pavement within view of the classroom window while Rachel assisted Ian with his remedial work. Tom had started driving her and Jimmy to and from school in an effort to ensure their safety. There had been no more incidents at the house since the mouse. She only wished Tom's efforts would work equally well on her school prankster.

After going through all Ian's work and assigning a couple of tasks for homework, Rachel said, "You're doing well. I'm proud of you."

Ian's cheeks reddened. He mumbled his thanks and quickly gathered his books.

The moment the teen left the classroom, Tom came in. "Ready to go?"

"Almost." Rachel stuffed her daily planner and books into her book bag and locked her desk drawers.

"How was your day?" he asked.

Everything she'd kept bottled up inside suddenly erupted like a volcano. "It's been one thing after another. Yesterday the test papers. Today my library reservation was canceled. And I know I scheduled it for today, not in a week. Someone's trying to make me seem incompetent. And the worst thing is, he's succeeding. The principal always seems to be around to notice when things go wrong."

Tom closed the distance between them and pulled her into an embrace. "Everything will be okay. You're a good teacher, and he knows it."

The warmth in his voice and the gentle pressure of his arms enfolding her chipped away at her frustration. "I'm starting to doubt myself and question whether I really booked the library on the wrong day. I feel like I'm losing my mind."

"If Ellen or someone else who's jealous of your position is behind these things, that might be exactly what they're hoping to accomplish."

"I refuse to give them the satisfaction," Rachel said.

He released her and stepped back. "That's the spirit."

For a moment, they gazed at each other, and Rachel's promise to Charlene flitted through her mind.

"Where are Katy and Jimmy?" Tom asked.

She shook the thought from her mind and pointed to the window. "Outside."

"I've been monitoring Blake's whereabouts the past couple of days," he commented. "Unless he's doing so remotely or through his son, he couldn't have switched the test masters or erased the library schedule."

Rachel sighed. "The test mistake could simply have been an error on the secretary's part. And anyone who can access the school's scheduling system could have changed the dates on my library reservation."

"Is that something Blake could do as a guest teacher here?"

"Yes. But if Richard's paying Blake to make me look bad enough to lose my job, why play nice and lend me his Range Rover?"

"To avert suspicion."

She frowned. "That makes sense."

"Ellen has a strong motive to make you appear incompetent too."

"Let's go," Rachel said, rubbing her temples. "I don't want to think about this anymore."

The next morning breezed by without so much as a hiccup. Maybe between the car fire and the message on her porch, Rachel had gotten a bit too paranoid and read something more into the test mishap and the missing library reservation.

By afternoon, she started to let her guard down, and her class enjoyed a boisterous learning session in the garden. They returned to the classroom for the final hour so she could demonstrate the day's math lesson on the whiteboard.

Rachel wrote down the data they'd collected outside and the formulas they needed for their calculations. When she did an example with the class, an astute student pointed out an error. "Good catch," she commended and grabbed the eraser. She swiped at the number that needed correcting, but nothing happened. She tried again. Still nothing.

She swiped at other numbers. None of them would wipe off.

Laughter rose among the students.

Rachel picked up the marker she'd been using—the marker left on the whiteboard's ledge. Bold letters on the barrel read: *permanent ink*. "Who put this marker here?"

No one spoke up.

She studied each student, hoping to detect who was hiding something. But she couldn't spot a guilty countenance among them. "These pranks have to stop. Whiteboards aren't cheap. The cost to replace this board will come out of funds raised for our class trips. I'll insist on it. Unless the culprit comes forward and takes responsibility for the cost."

The students remained silent. Any hope peer pressure would compel a confession quickly faded.

The instant the bell rang, her students escaped without another word. Katy alone remained at her desk. "What are you going to do?"

"Take rubbing alcohol to the board," Rachel answered. "That should remove the ink. But I'll have to report it to the principal."

"I don't think any of your students switched the marker," Katy said. "At least I didn't hear anyone snickering about it like they usually do when they play a joke on someone."

"That's good to know." Rachel sighed. "Unfortunately, anyone could have slipped into the classroom while we were outside." Both Ellen and Blake were at school today. At least this proved that the new rash of pranks hadn't been her overactive imagination.

Principal Sutton marched into the classroom. "I heard you used a permanent marker on the whiteboard."

So Rachel had a prankster and a tattletale. "Yes, someone replaced my dry-erase marker with a permanent one, and I didn't notice until it was too late."

The principal frowned. "Trouble seems determined to find you on a daily basis."

"Yes sir," Rachel conceded.

"You can't allow your students to get the best of you," Mr. Sutton advised. "Take a firm hand with them from the beginning. Otherwise, they'll be walking all over you by Christmas, and you'll never regain authority."

"Yes sir." What else could Rachel say? Everything he said was true. If she admitted that she wasn't sure her culprit was a student, it would only make her seem paranoid. She could convince him that she wasn't if she told him about the incidents at her house. She mulled over the option. What if he suspected she had a stalker? He might worry about her students' safety and place her on leave until the culprit was caught.

She couldn't afford that. But should she be worried for her students' safety? Surely someone with an inexplicable grudge against her wouldn't take it out on her students.

Would they?

By Friday afternoon, Tom had run out of ideas for how to nab whoever was harassing Rachel, short of entrapment.

After dropping off his sister at home, he parked in Rachel's driveway. The security cameras he'd mounted around her property had yet to capture any uninvited visitors. The Boston PI he'd hired to investigate Rachel's brother-in-law hadn't uncovered anything they didn't already know. And the evidence he had to implicate either Ellen or Blake in the pranks at the school and the other incidents was circumstantial at best.

If he'd put up the security cameras before the mouse incident, he would have seen the culprit in the act. Waiting for the person to act again was not how Tom wanted to catch him or her.

He opened the truck's back door to let Jimmy out. "I'm afraid you'll have to drive yourself to school next week," he said to Rachel. "I'm on afternoon shifts." His driving her had seemed to work as a deterrent, but how long would that last once she was on her own?

"Steven Holman, the father of one of the teachers at work, is selling his Jeep," she responded. "He's going to bring it by for me to test-drive tomorrow morning."

"Do you mind if I check it over too?"

"I'd be happy if you would. But won't you be fishing?"

"No, fishing tonight should give me my fill." He grinned at Jimmy. "Right?"

Jimmy beamed. Fishing was all he'd talked about since Tom had volunteered to take him out.

Rachel dug her house key out of her purse. "I'll change and pack the snacks I made for us."

Tom snagged Jimmy's backpack from the back seat. "You'll want to take this in."

"Is his baseball cap still in the truck?" she asked.

"No, it's here." Tom reached into the bag and pulled out a Boston Red Sox cap.

A piece of paper folded to the size of a business card tumbled to the ground.

Tom retrieved the paper and opened it. Scanning the single typewritten sentence, he bit back a curse. When had someone slipped this note into Jimmy's bag?

"What's wrong?" Rachel asked, tension lacing her voice.

Rather than read the contents aloud, Tom turned the paper for Rachel to see. Her tortured expression wrenched his heart.

Clenching his fists, Tom silently reread the message.

I was this close to your son.

20

Jimmy hopped from foot to foot, oblivious to the magnitude of the note Rachel had just read. "Hurry and get changed," he told her. "It'll be too dark to fish soon."

"I think we might have to plan to go another day instead." Rachel searched Tom's features, wondering if he agreed. She imagined he'd try to lift fingerprints from the note in hopes to find something that might give them a clue as to who had planted it.

Tom's grimace said he hated to disappoint Jimmy.

Thunder rumbled.

"I'm afraid your mom's right," Tom said. "We can't fish in a thunderstorm. It's too dangerous."

"No," Jimmy whined.

"Don't worry," Tom said, ruffling Jimmy's hair. "We'll go fishing again soon."

"Tom can still join us for supper." Rachel faced Tom. "If you want to, that is."

"I'd like that." More quietly, he said, "Perhaps you could distract Jimmy with a TV show or the computer while I run tests on the note?"

Relieved, she nodded, then ushered them into the house. Soon Jimmy was watching his favorite cartoon.

Rachel retreated to the kitchen, where Tom was pressing his thumb onto a blank card. "What are you doing?"

"I found prints on the note. But I have to eliminate mine." Tom wiped his inked fingers clean, then put on a pair of latex gloves. He examined the note with a magnifying glass, his gaze shifting periodically to the fingerprint card he'd created. "The lone thumbprint on the written side belongs to me." He turned the page over. "But these prints on the back, which were most likely made when the page was folded, belong to someone else. When was the last time you emptied Jimmy's backpack?"

"I can't remember," she admitted. "Probably sometime last week."

"So this note could have been placed in the bag anytime within the past week or more," he concluded.

"I suppose so." To handle her escalating fears for Jimmy's safety, Rachel distracted herself by opening the fridge to figure out what to prepare for supper. "Richard had access to the backpack last week."

"Did he have access to a printer?"

"Perhaps at his rental cottage. Could you get in and compare a printout from it to this one?"

"If I can reach the owner of the house for permission," Tom said. "And if that printer is one of the color laser printers that has a Machine Identification Code, or MIC, which they print on every page so that you can identify which printer they came from. Otherwise, I don't think comparing printouts will lead us to the right person, since printouts tend to look the same no matter which printer they came from. Richard also spent time doing repairs here, so the printout might very well match your own printer's MIC."

"Well, if it does, then we'd know for sure Richard planted it." She pulled a worksheet from her binder that she'd printed the night before. "This is from my printer. I'm afraid there's nothing terribly distinctive about the letters."

He held his magnifying glass to the page. "Actually, there is something. See the *y*?"

Rachel scanned the words and zeroed in on a *y*. "It seems to overlap a little with the *o* beside it."

"Exactly. That usually means a printer has an outdated driver. It's not as likely to be widespread." Tom shifted the magnifying glass to the note from Jimmy's backpack. "This one doesn't have that issue."

She shook her head. "Richard didn't print it. At least, not from my printer."

"Unless, like you said, he printed it at the cottage he was renting or had someone else print it for him," he reasoned. "I think I know how we can compare his fingerprints."

"How?"

Tom disappeared into the mudroom and returned a moment later with a toolbox. "I saw Richard using this when he fixed your drain." He dusted the handle and the lid. "I have a good sample of the thumb and index finger of each hand here."

Rachel put a pot of water on the stove to boil for spaghetti while Tom worked.

"The prints on the back of the page don't belong to Richard," he announced.

Not sure whether to be frustrated or relieved, Rachel busied herself with setting the table. "Any number of people at the school could have put the note in Jimmy's backpack. It's clearly labeled, so anyone who saw it would know it belonged to my son."

"I should be able to surreptitiously secure clean fingerprints from our suspects without much trouble," Tom said. "I'm thinking Ellen, Blake, and Ian to begin with, and we can see if their printers have MICs."

"You don't need a warrant?"

"I would if it was an official search," he answered. "You could request a typed report from Ian. A peek at a quote from Blake's office should take care of another printer available to him."

"Any page Ellen preps for her classes would allow us to assess hers," she added.

"Exactly. As for fingerprints, any cup they've handled and discarded will supply those."

"I can't believe Ian would do these things," Rachel commented. "He seems like a really nice kid, and he's grateful that I've helped him learn ways to overcome his learning difficulties."

"And you've given Blake what he wanted too," Tom said. "You're allowing his son to play football."

"Unless Richard lied about why he paid him," she theorized. "Although Blake did caulk the windows this week."

"Still, the two are old friends," he reminded her. "The job might have been for the sake of appearances."

Jimmy appeared in the doorway. "When's supper? I'm hungry."

"It's almost ready," Rachel answered. "You can go wash up."

Jimmy dashed off.

"I don't want to believe Richard is behind everything," she said. "But despite the doting uncle performance he gave last week, he's the only one with a strong motive to scare me out of my job and home."

"It's time I confront him and demand answers," Tom said. "I could take the late ferry into Boston tonight and return on the first one in the morning."

Rachel shivered at the thought of what could happen while Tom was off the island.

As if he'd read her mind, he said, "Or better yet, I can ask my PI buddy to speak to him."

She chewed on her bottom lip. "If Richard is innocent, the last thing I want to do is give him another reason to be angry with me. Could we wait until you eliminate Ellen's and Blake's fingerprints and printers?"

"Sure," Tom said. "I'll ask each of them outright. Because the note threatened Jimmy, they shouldn't hesitate to provide me with fingerprints and a sample from their printers to prove their innocence."

"Are you sure you want them to know about the evidence you have?" Rachel asked. "They could deliberately mislead you by using a different printer."

Jimmy returned to the kitchen.

Tom held Rachel's gaze a moment longer. "I'll be thorough," he said quietly.

After offering him a small smile of appreciation, she set the pot of spaghetti in the center of the table.

A knock sounded at the back door.

Startled, Rachel jumped, then stared at Tom in alarm.

"Stay here," he whispered as he rose and walked toward the door.

She lurched from her chair to shield Jimmy.

The door opened, and Richard entered the kitchen. "Do I smell spaghetti?"

Jimmy bounced up and made a beeline for his uncle. "You came back!"

Tom subtly motioned with his hand for Rachel to stay calm.

"I wasn't expecting you," Rachel said to Richard.

"I felt bad for the way I rushed off on Jimmy last weekend." Richard scooped up Jimmy and hugged him. "I figured we could get in that fishing trip I promised you tomorrow."

"Yay!" Jimmy yelled.

"How did you get here?" she asked Richard, trying to sound nonchalant.

"I caught a cab from the airport."

"Have you had dinner yet?" Rachel asked. "We have plenty if you'd like to eat with us."

"That would be great." Richard put Jimmy down, then removed his coat.

She set another place at the table for him.

Tom switched places with Rachel, conveniently placing himself between her and Richard. "We were just talking about you."

Rachel felt the blood drain from her face.

"All good, I hope." Richard grinned.

"Did you leave a note for me in Jimmy's backpack last week?" she asked.

"No," Richard said. Nothing in his tone betrayed his emotions. "What was it about?"

Rachel carefully twirled spaghetti onto her fork. "We can discuss that after Jimmy goes to bed."

"I have a few things I need to discuss with you too," Richard said.

Jimmy frowned. "I don't have to go to bed yet, do I?"

"Of course not," Richard assured him.

She bristled at his presumption to answer on her behalf.

The rest of the meal was almost pleasant. Richard focused on his nephew, and Jimmy reveled in the attention. But by the time Rachel put Jimmy to bed, the atmosphere seemed to be charged with a current that had nothing to do with the thunderstorm flashing lightning outside.

Rachel left Jimmy's bedroom and joined the two men in the living room.

Tom handed Richard the note in a sealed evidence bag.

"I didn't write this," Richard declared. He set the note on the coffee table. "But I understand why you thought I might have. I've been a complete slimeball."

Surprisingly relieved that her concerns were out in the open so quickly, Rachel chuckled at Richard's expressive choice of words.

"I swear I didn't write that note." Richard hung his head. "But I confess that I did sign into the house's smart system on your first day of school to make the lights and TV come on."

Rachel sucked in a breath.

"I was trying to spook you out of wanting to stay here," Richard admitted. "After I heard how much my prank had frightened Jimmy, I felt terrible for being so childish. And too ashamed to own up to it."

"But not ashamed enough to put the brakes on your plans to scare her off the island," Tom accused.

"No! The fire and the other things you mentioned weren't my doing." Richard turned to Rachel. "You have to believe me."

She raised an eyebrow, feeling far from ready to believe anything he said.

Richard emitted a heavy sigh. "After the way I've acted since my parents' deaths, compounded by these other crazy things that have been happening to you, I can't blame you for being wary."

Rachel folded her arms over her chest.

"I admit that before my last visit to the island, I asked Blake to keep me informed of your actions," Richard continued.

"So you asked him to spy on me," she said. And to think she'd believed Blake when he told her at the Grandparents' Day event that he hadn't realized she was James's widow.

Richard nodded. "My actions were stupid. I know there's no excuse, but please understand that none of this was because I have anything against you."

Rachel scoffed. "It sure doesn't feel that way."

"I was consumed with guilt over my parents' deaths," Richard said. "The accident was my fault."

"What do you mean?" she asked.

"I was supposed to come to Martha's Vineyard that weekend, but something came up and I canceled my trip," Richard explained. "Saturday was my birthday, so Mom and Dad decided to visit me in Boston to celebrate. If I had come to them as planned, they wouldn't have been on the road, and maybe they'd still be here." He paused. "I suppose lashing out at you was my inept way of trying to deal with my guilt."

Rachel's heart wrenched. She actually believed him this time. Guilt was an old friend of hers—both in her husband's death and her in-laws'. She and Jimmy were supposed to go to Boston with her in-laws, but Jimmy had woken with a fever that morning, which had delayed their departure.

For weeks following the accident, she'd been plagued with what-ifs. What if she'd been driving? Or what if she hadn't belabored the decision to stay home and delayed their departure? Tears threatened to spill down her cheeks, and Tom squeezed her hand. He'd been her one beacon of hope through all of this.

"It wasn't your fault," Rachel told Richard. "You can't blame yourself."

Richard blew his nose and swiped at his own damp eyes. "I'm grateful that at least God spared you and Jimmy that day. I don't know what I would do if I lost both of you too."

Although Rachel still had questions about Richard, she couldn't ignore his heartfelt words. She got up and sat next to him on the sofa, then placed a comforting hand on his shoulder.

Richard patted her hand. "I've withdrawn my appeal of the judge's decision on my parents' will."

For a moment, Rachel was speechless. Then she gave her brother-in-law a hug and whispered, "Thank you."

"I don't know what I was thinking," Richard said. "I shouldn't have contested my parents' will, and I should have focused on helping my brother's widow. I'm so sorry."

They sat in silence for a few moments. Rachel felt as if a burden had been lifted from her shoulders.

"Someone is still threatening Rachel and Jimmy," Tom said, breaking the silence. "Are you certain it's not Blake?"

"Positive," Richard answered. "I was telling the truth when I told you I hired him to do repairs on the place." He faced Rachel. "I thought you were making mountains out of molehills with the other things that had been happening. I figured I'd scared you so much with my signing into your smart system that you were seeing malicious intent behind fluke accidents like the car fire and schoolboy pranks."

"The fire wasn't an accident," Tom said firmly. "And especially after this note, I'm not convinced the supposed pranks are the work of a student."

"I swear I wasn't behind the fire or any of the other incidents," Richard insisted. "I would never frighten Jimmy with a phone call or write this note." He motioned to the note on the coffee table, his voice rising with indignation. "What kind of monster would terrorize a little boy?"

One that's still out there, Rachel thought.

21

The next morning, Tom went over to Rachel's house as soon as he spotted movement on the main floor. "I hope you don't mind my coming by so early. I wanted to talk to you before Richard arrived."

"What is it?" Rachel asked. "Did you learn something else?" Anxiety colored her voice, and he regretted adding to her fear.

"No, nothing like that. But last night as I was rehashing our conversation with Richard, I wondered if Blake had seen something significant while spying on you." Tom opted not to mention that he'd also still like to rule out Blake's fingerprints and printer in connection with the note left in Jimmy's backpack.

"We should go speak to him on our way to this morning's fishing spot," she suggested. "I think he'd be more forthcoming with Richard there, urging him to be completely honest."

"Good idea," he said. It also occurred to him that if Richard hadn't been completely honest with them last night, he'd be forced to feign his support in front of Blake, so that either way the man shouldn't hold anything back. "When are you expecting Richard?"

Rachel checked her watch. "Not for an hour. Steven Holman is bringing me the Jeep to test-drive in twenty minutes, so I'd better wake Jimmy. We still have to eat breakfast."

"Okay, I'll be back then."

Thirty minutes later, Tom closed the hood on Steven's pristine Jeep, then slid underneath the vehicle. It clearly had an undercoating, because despite being a decade old, there was minimal rust. Tom slid back out. "The brake lines and gas line look good. The rocker panels are solid, and the muffler isn't too bad." He accepted a rag from Rachel and wiped the grease from his hands. "Ready to take it for a spin?"

"If you think it's safe." She sounded nervous, which was only natural, given the fact that her last car had burst into flames.

"It's safe," he assured her.

Tom and Jimmy climbed into the back so Steven could ride up front with Rachel.

As she drove around the back roads, she deliberately swerved to test the handling, then came to an abrupt stop to test the brakes.

"That was fun," Jimmy said. "Do it again!"

Steven chuckled.

Rachel glanced in the rearview mirror, meeting Tom's gaze, and they exchanged smiles.

After a few more laps around the block and a couple in a nearby parking lot—which Jimmy thought was even more fun—they returned to the house.

"I'll take it," Rachel told Steven as they climbed out of the Jeep.

"Great. My new vehicle doesn't arrive until next Tuesday or Wednesday. Would it be all right if we take care of the sale after that? That will give me time to get the paperwork together."

Rachel agreed, and Steven made his leave.

Richard arrived as the man drove out of sight. "Who was that?"

"The owner of the Jeep I'm buying," Rachel answered.

"What?" Richard asked, sounding offended. "Why didn't you let me—"

"No need," she interrupted. "Tom checked over the body and engine for me. It's a good deal."

He felt a swell of pride at her trust in him.

"I love it!" Jimmy exclaimed, adding his vote of confidence. "Mommy could do doughnuts in the parking lot with it."

Richard laughed. "I suppose that's the most important thing. Now are we ready to go fishing?"

"The gear's loaded," Tom said.

"Let me grab our cooler." Rachel dashed inside and returned with a soft-sided cooler bag. "We're all going in Tom's truck," she informed Richard.

"I don't mind driving too," Richard said, climbing into the back seat beside Jimmy.

"That's okay," she responded, apparently still not ready to trust him completely. "It's silly to take two vehicles when we all fit in this one."

Tom smiled at her riding shotgun beside him. He was glad Richard was riding with them. He didn't want to give the man a chance to coach Blake on his responses before they arrived. "We have to make a stop on the way," he informed Richard.

They drove to a campground and found Blake's truck parked on one of the roads that wound through it.

Rachel pointed to the roof of a house. "There he is."

"What do you want with Blake?" Richard asked.

"Since you hired him to do repairs on the cottage," Tom said, "we wanted to ask him if he'd seen anyone lurking around while he was there."

"Let's see what he says." Richard shot out of the truck. "Hey, Blake, can you come down? We need to talk to you for a few minutes."

Tom and Rachel quickly flanked Richard before Blake could join him.

Blake gave instructions to another worker on the roof, then descended a nearby ladder. "What's going on?"

"Remember when I asked you to keep an eye on Rachel?" Richard asked.

Blake glanced at Rachel, and his face reddened.

"Don't worry," Richard assured him. "She knows."

Tom smirked. *Keeping an eye on Rachel* wasn't the same as doing a few repairs on the cottage.

"We're hoping you can help us," Richard continued. "We need to know if you saw anything out of the ordinary, such as anyone nosing around her place or following her."

Blake gazed skyward, as if searching the recesses of his mind. "Not really, no."

"Are you sure?" Tom urged. "Anything at all?"

"Well, Drew pulled into her driveway the day I was caulking the windows," Blake replied.

"Drew?" Tom asked.

"I don't know his first name," Blake said. "Mr. Drew, the school custodian. He rolled down his car window and asked me what I was up to."

"Jack knows about some of the pranks that have been played on me at school," Rachel said. "He was probably making sure you weren't up to any mischief."

"But what was he doing passing your house in the first place?" Richard asked. "For that matter, how did he know which house was yours?"

"He lives about a mile up the road from us," Tom said. "Did you notice anyone else skulking about the place?"

"No," Blake said. "Never."

Tom thanked Blake for his time, then drove them to the beach to fish from one of the jetties. The surrounding waters were a prime spot for false albacore and bonitos, so during derby time, the jetties on either end of the bridge were crowded with surf casters and fly fishermen.

"I didn't expect to see so many people," Rachel commented. "Where are you going to park?"

"We might have a bit of a hike." Tom spotted the blip of a turn signal on a car parked along the road up ahead and managed to slide into the spot the driver vacated. He grinned at Jimmy in the rearview mirror. "How's that for timing?"

Jimmy's giggle dispelled the shadow that had seemed to settle over their little group since chatting with Blake.

They collected their gear from the back and headed for the longer jetty on the other side of the bridge. Jimmy skipped along the giant boulders, obviously eager to find a prime fishing spot. In places, the fishermen were so numerous that they stood practically shoulder to shoulder.

Midway up the jetty, a kindly older gentleman gathered his belongings and invited them to take his spot.

As Tom prepared Jimmy's rod, Rachel picked her way down the opposite side of the jetty toward the sand. "I'm going to search for sea glass along the beach."

Tom handed Jimmy his rod and headed her off. "I don't think that's a good idea."

She stared at him in alarm. "Why not?"

"We should stick together," Tom explained. "I can't monitor both you and Jimmy if you're in two different places."

Rachel stiffened. "You think we could be in danger with all these people around?"

"It's possible," Tom said. "We don't know who left the note. We don't know if he actually intends harm or if he's playing mind games. If Ellen wrote the note, then I'd suspect the latter. But I can't rule out that you have a stalker."

"Now you're really scaring me," she said, rubbing her arms.

"That's not my intention," Tom said. "But I would feel a lot more relaxed if you stuck close."

"I can do that," Rachel said, her voice softening.

A sudden shout of excitement rang out.

Rachel scrambled back up the slanted rocks of the side of the jetty. "What's that?"

Grinning, Tom pointed to a nearby fisherman. "He caught a fish, and it's making a run for it."

Everyone along the jetty watched, calling encouragement and advice.

"That's so cool," Jimmy exclaimed, watching the fisherman reel in the albacore. "I hope I catch one of those."

The next hour passed pleasantly. Around them the swish of fly fishermen's lines punctuated fishermen's tales of their last big catch or the even bigger catch that got away. Seagulls swooped and squawked, and the rhythmic sound of the water breaking on the rocks soothed the soul. For his part, Jimmy got a few nibbles on his line. Richard reeled in a decent fluke, which he immediately released.

A group of elderly gentlemen strolled by.

"Seen any action?" a familiar voice asked.

Rachel greeted Jack Drew and his companions.

"A couple of boils," Tom answered. "A few guys hooked up, but there haven't been any keepers yet."

"Same scenario at the fishing pier," one of the men remarked.

Tom suddenly noticed that Jack's coat had a tear—and that it was constructed of the same material he'd found in the parking lot where Rachel's car had been parked before it caught fire. "How did you rip your jacket?" he asked the custodian.

Jack glanced down and poked an arthritic finger at the tear. "That? I sliced it with a box cutter while unpacking supplies at the school."

Tom cocked his head. The damage was clearly a tear, not a clean cut made by a sharp knife. "Do you wear your jacket when you're working inside? Unpacking boxes, I mean."

"Sometimes," Jack said. His tone verged on defensive.

All at once the disconnected pieces clicked together. Jack was the custodian, so it would have been easy for him to pull the pranks on Rachel at school and plant the notes. And he lived less than a mile from her house. He clearly monitored her comings and goings, as evidenced by his questioning Blake. But why didn't he want her on the island?

The squash. Ellen said her father lived not far from Tom. "You wouldn't happen to be Ellen Donovan's father, would you?"

"So?" Jack asked, studying him.

Tom clenched his jaw. If he'd done his job and searched for the address of Ellen's father, he would have realized that there was no Mr. Donovan in his neighborhood and made the connection two weeks ago. He pushed aside his annoyance with himself and offered Jack a nonchalant shrug. "Ellen mentioned her father had a bumper crop of squash this year, but I didn't realize that was you because you have different last names."

"She took her mother's name after the divorce," Jack groused.

Rachel stared at Tom. She'd clearly made the connection now too.

Tom motioned to the tear in Jack's coat. "Looks as if a piece of fabric was torn off. Hard to believe a box cutter would cause that."

"No matter." Jack wrapped the other jacket flap over the torn side and started down the jetty.

"But it does matter," Tom said, raising his voice a fraction. "I'm sure you remember that I found a similar piece of fabric where Rachel's car was parked—the car that caught on fire a couple of hours later."

Jack whirled around. His left eye twitched. "What are you implying?"

"I thought it was obvious," Tom said.

Jack glanced from side to side, as if he were searching for an escape from the crowded jetty.

Tom caught the old man by the arm. "I think you have some explaining to do."

Jack wrenched his arm free of Tom's grasp, then shoved Jimmy toward the water before leaping off the opposite side of the jetty to the sand.

Jimmy's scream split the air. Then the boy hit the rocks with a sickening thud.

22

Jimmy tumbled into the water.

With a shriek, Rachel lunged for her son.

Tom caught her arm and shoved her toward Richard. "Stay here." He stripped off his coat and skidded midway down the sloping rocks before diving into the water after her little boy.

Rachel watched in horror as Jimmy bobbed to the surface, one arm flailing, the other nowhere to be seen, then disappeared again. Seconds later, he reappeared yards away.

"The current is pulling him out to sea!" someone shouted.

Around them every fisherman on the jetty reeled in their lines. Dozens of people pressed their phones to their ears.

Next to her, Richard called 911.

Her legs turned to jelly, and Rachel prayed, *God, please don't let my son die.*

Richard finished the call and held on to her, keeping her steady. "He'll be okay. Don't worry. Tom has almost reached him already."

Tom's muscular arms and powerful kicks sliced through the water, eating up the distance between him and Jimmy.

"Hang on, Jimmy!" Rachel called. A sob muffled his name in her throat. She broke free of Richard's grasp and ran along the jetty to stay alongside them.

With one powerful kick, Tom surged forward and caught her son.

"He's not moving," she said to Richard, who was keeping pace beside her. "Oh no, he's not moving! Please, Lord, not my son too!"

With Jimmy tucked under one arm, Tom did a sidestroke toward the jetty.

"It's too difficult to bring him up this way," someone murmured.

A couple of fishermen edged down the slick sloping rocks as another one waded into the water to give Tom a hand.

Rachel pushed past the people lining the jetty. "Is he okay?"

Behind her, Richard bellowed, "Make way! That's her son."

"Is the boy breathing?" a woman yelled.

Tom raised his head. "Yes, he's breathing."

"Then it'll be quicker for you to swim around the end of the jetty to the beach," the woman advised. "The paramedics can meet you there with a stretcher."

Tom consulted the man who'd joined him in the water. A moment later, Tom redirected his strokes toward the end of the jetty.

"The harbormaster's boat is on the way," someone reported.

"He'll have the boy out of the water before the boat gets here," another said.

Rachel jogged along the jetty, staying level with Tom and her son. "Mommy's here, Jimmy. Hold on. You'll be okay."

The shriek of sirens pierced the air. Fire trucks, police cruisers, and an ambulance sped toward them.

Richard grabbed Rachel's arm and steered her off the jetty onto the sand. They raced for the beach.

Paramedics hurried up behind them with a stretcher, and police officers descended on the beach.

The crowd cheered when Tom gained his feet, cradling Jimmy in his arms.

Rachel dashed through the shallows to their side. "I'm here, honey. Mommy's here."

Jimmy's lips were blue and quivering, and his wet hair was plastered to his forehead. But his eyes fluttered open, and he managed a little grin. "Tom saved me, just like Superman."

Rachel laughed, her tears flowing freely now. "He sure did." She stroked the hair from her son's forehead and kissed his cheek. "He's our very own superhero."

A paramedic carefully lifted Jimmy from Tom's arms, placed him on a stretcher, and draped a blanket over him.

"I think his arm is broken," Tom cautioned.

Rachel shuddered at the scrapes visible beneath Jimmy's torn sleeve and pant leg.

The paramedics instantly began assessing her boy. "Pupils equal and reactive. Pulse is good. Respiration good."

Rachel gave Tom a hug. "Thank you."

He clasped her arms and stepped back. "I don't want to get water all over your clothes."

"I'm not worried about it. I almost lost Jimmy," Rachel whispered. "But you saved him." She got on her tiptoes and kissed him. His lips were warm and salty and so very soft.

He slid his fingers through her hair and cupped the back of her head, drawing her closer as he deepened the kiss.

Her heart thundered. She felt as if she were plummeting off the jetty and Tom was the only one who could save her.

He kissed her again, then rested his forehead against hers and smiled.

Rachel returned his smile. Suddenly self-conscious, she glanced around. If seeing her kiss Tom bothered Richard, he didn't show it. Jimmy seemed pleased as punch, with his mile-wide grin.

A paramedic placed a blanket over Tom's shoulders. "We've stabilized the boy's arm, and we're ready to transport him. Do you want to ride with him to the hospital? We need to check you over too."

Tom straightened, his professional demeanor sliding back into place. "Let his mother go with him. I'll follow in my truck."

"Are you okay to drive?" the paramedic asked.

"I'll drive him," Richard volunteered.

A cop escorted them as they trekked beside the paramedics up the sand to the road. "A police officer will meet you at the hospital to question you about the accident."

"This was no accident," Richard declared. "The janitor pushed Jimmy so he could get away."

"Janitor?" the officer repeated.

"Jack Drew," Tom clarified. "He's the school custodian."

"And he's been harassing my sister-in-law ever since she started working at the school," Richard interjected. "He's crazy."

"I suspect that Jack was hoping to scare Rachel into quitting so that his daughter would get the position the school hired Rachel to fill." Tom gave the other officer a rundown of the offenses Jack had allegedly committed. "I don't know if Ellen helped her father."

"I'll phone the police station and have them send an officer to Mr. Drew's house," the cop promised.

Rachel drank in the sight of her son, looking so small under the blanket on the stretcher. She couldn't believe that Jimmy had almost died over Jack's resentment of her getting the teaching position.

She fervently thanked God for giving Jimmy back to her and ending this nightmare once and for all.

Two hours later, after grabbing takeout for lunch, Tom helped Rachel and Richard settle Jimmy at the house. "I'm going to call Beckett for an update," he said to Rachel and slipped into the kitchen to make the call in private. He'd expected them to have Jack Drew in custody by now. The fact he was still on the loose didn't bode well.

"We found no sign of the suspect at his house," Officer Beckett reported to Tom. "We've confirmed he doesn't own a boat. The BOLO on his car and the alert at the ferry terminals haven't netted any results yet."

Rachel padded into the kitchen and searched his face expectantly.

"Keep me updated," Tom said into the phone. He disconnected the call, then took Rachel's hands in his. He'd hoped to be able to tell her that her troubles were over. "I'm afraid Jack Drew is on the run. Now that you and Jimmy are home safe and sound, I think I should pay Ellen a visit."

"But what if he comes here?" she asked, fear evident in her voice.

"He won't," Tom declared with utter certainty about that at least. "Jack knows every cop on the island is searching for him after what he did to Jimmy. There's no way he'd risk coming here. No, our best hope of finding him is to convince his daughter to tell us where he might hide on the island or who might help him escape."

Rachel lifted her chin. "I'm coming with you."

"Are you sure you want to leave Jimmy?"

Rachel watched Jimmy playing a game with his uncle in the living room. "He won't mind." She squeezed Tom's hands and gave him a heart-stopping smile. "Thanks to you, he seems no worse for wear for his tumble. He's quite proud of his cast."

"He's a great kid."

She smiled even brighter. "I think so, but I could be biased. Give me a minute. I'll meet you outside."

He exited the house and walked to his truck, then leaned against it as he waited.

A few minutes later, Rachel joined him. "Richard's happy to stay with Jimmy."

Tom opened the passenger door for her. "Would it be awful to admit that in one way I'll be sad to see this case close? I won't have an excuse to come over every day."

Rachel's cheeks flushed a lovely shade of pink.

He tilted his head. "Then again, once the case is closed, I won't have to worry about a conflict of interest."

"Conflict of interest?" she echoed.

This was not the time to revisit their amazing kiss and what it had meant to him. "A discussion best kept for later."

Not that the postponement kept his heart from thundering during the entire drive to Ellen's house. The warmth and loveliness in Rachel's expression had left him tongue-tied, and he wasn't sure he could string two intelligible words together anyway. Somewhere between being swept into her arms on the beach and watching her hold her son's hand in the hospital, Tom had come to the realization that he couldn't imagine his life without Rachel—and not just as his neighbor and friend.

Tom shook his head in wonder at how his feelings for Rachel had vanquished every reservation he'd ever had about getting involved in a serious relationship. Even if she wanted more children—he realized he was getting way ahead of himself here—he was willing to take that risk. Coping with Katy's developmental delays and health problems had been hard on his parents, but he couldn't have asked for a better sister. All their lives were richer because of her.

Life was a risky business—period. The best they could do was live each day to the fullest, with courage and kindness toward one another, the way his sister did.

His hands grew slick on the steering wheel. Tom stretched his fingers and peeked across the truck at Rachel. She was watching the passing scenery in silence. *Courage.* Rachel was the most courageous woman he knew. But would she have the courage to take another chance on love?

When they reached Ellen's driveway, Rachel gasped. "That's the car that was following Charlene and me. Is it Ellen's?"

"No." Tom scanned the license plate, confirming his suspicions. "It's her father's car. I can't believe patrols didn't spot him here." He parked crosswise at the end of the driveway to prevent Jack's escape.

"You think he'll try to run again?"

Tom arched an eyebrow, surprised she needed to ask.

They jumped out of the truck and headed to the front door.

Ellen stormed out of the house and propped her hands on her hips. "I hope you're not going to accuse me of something else I didn't do."

"No, we know the car fire was your father's doing," Tom responded. "May we speak to him?"

"What?" Ellen demanded. Her voice shot up two decibels. She glanced over her shoulder into the house.

Tom heard the back door slam shut and raced to the backyard.

Jack skidded to a halt and raised his hands in surrender. "Okay, I give up. I'm too old to run anymore."

Nevertheless, Tom secured him with handcuffs before escorting him around to the front of the house. He called dispatch to call off the BOLO and request a cruiser to pick up the man.

Ellen flew down the porch steps. "What's going on?"

"Leave my daughter out of this," Jack hissed under his breath to Tom. "She didn't know anything about what I was doing."

Ellen halted in front of her father and gaped. "What are you talking about?" Her gaze darted from Rachel to Tom and finally back to her dad. She gasped. "You didn't!"

Jack toed the dirt. "I might have gotten carried away."

"Carried away?" The exasperation in Ellen's voice was palpable. "You were behind all those childish pranks at the school?"

Jack shrugged.

"And you made that horrible call to Rachel's son too?" Ellen continued. "What were you thinking? He's a little boy."

"I wanted to scare the woman into quitting so you could claim the teaching job that should have been yours." Jack reached a hand toward his daughter, only then seeming to remember they were cuffed.

Ellen jumped back as if burned. "Did you think that would make up for what you did to Mom?"

Jack winced, but he didn't respond.

"I had no idea he was behind all those things," Ellen said to Tom. "I've barely talked to him since he divorced my mother."

"You see him every time you're at the school, and you got squash from him," Tom reminded her, allowing his skepticism to creep into his tone. "And you acted guilty when I questioned you about driving by Rachel's house."

Ellen snorted. "I was checking out your place. Looking to see if *you* were home."

Tom tried not to let his surprise show.

To her father, Ellen snapped, "The police thought I was responsible."

"I'm sorry," Jack said. "I had no idea anyone would suspect you."

"That's always been your problem, hasn't it?" Ellen spat. "You don't think."

Officer Beckett arrived and took Jack into custody.

"Wait," Ellen said. "What will he be charged with?"

"For starters, arson and assault causing bodily harm," Beckett replied.

Ellen stared at her father. "You assaulted Rachel?"

"Not her," Tom said. "He almost killed Rachel's son."

"I'm sorry about the kid," Jack said. "I didn't mean to push him off the jetty. I swear it was an accident."

"That was no accident." Tom clenched his fists, straining to keep his tone even. "You deliberately pushed the boy to aid your escape."

"I didn't mean for him to fall into the water," Jack insisted.

"Anyone with a conscience wouldn't have fled the scene," Rachel pointed out. "You should have stuck around to help rescue my son."

"I'm sorry about Jimmy." Although anguish crossed Ellen's face, revulsion still tainted the glare she directed at her father. "He's mentally ill. He hasn't been himself in a long time."

"That will be for a judge to decide." Beckett led Jack to the cruiser.

"Come on." Tom rested his hand on the small of Rachel's back. "Let's go home."

23

Sunday evening, Rachel and Jimmy saw Richard off at the ferry, then accompanied Tom to the beach for a sunset picnic. As soon as Jimmy had finished eating, he set to work building a sandcastle.

Rachel stretched out her legs, leaned back, and propped herself up on her elbows. "Now, *this* is how living on an island is supposed to feel."

Tom smiled. "I agree."

They sat in companionable silence for a few moments.

"I'm sorry it took me so long to realize Jack was behind all the harassment," he said.

"It's not your fault," she said. "He never even occurred to me as a suspect, and I saw him every day."

"You know what they say—no one ever notices the help," Tom pointed out. "That's how the butler always gets away with the crime."

"I guess I need to brush up on my detective stories." Rachel shook her head. "Now that I think about it, something Blake said should have tipped me off."

"What did he say?"

"That a parent would do anything to see his child succeed."

"Even when that child is all grown up. But we didn't know that Ellen was Jack's daughter." Tom collected the empty takeout containers. "I went to the police station this afternoon to review the case against Jack while you and Jimmy were visiting with Richard."

"Did you learn anything new?" she asked.

"Jack confessed to tampering with your sprinklers and pulling all the pranks at school," Tom said, "except for the test mix-up, which was likely a mistake on the secretary's part."

Rachel remembered something else. "Was Jack the one who coaxed the little girl into blaming Jimmy for the food fight?"

"Jack did mention a food fight," he answered. "He also admitted to the phone call to Jimmy, the notes, and the dead mouse."

"Did he follow me and Charlene?"

Tom nodded. "Apparently Jack overheard the principal commend you on the compliments parents had been sharing with him. He figured he needed to step up his efforts to scare you off. And of course, he admitted to tampering with your car."

"Did he key Richard's SUV too?" she asked, then cringed when she recalled how she'd lashed out at Ellen at the hospital. "I need to apologize to Ellen for how I treated her. She must be upset with me, especially after she gave up her Saturday to stay with Jimmy."

"Your tormentor turned out to be her father, so Ellen can probably understand why you couldn't trust her," Tom said. "She called me and confessed to keying the SUV."

"Why didn't she call me?"

"Ellen was too ashamed," he said. "She promised to apologize to you personally, and she offered to pay for the damage. Do you want to press charges?"

"No, I wouldn't want it to cost her teaching hours at school," Rachel answered. "It sounds as if she needs all the work she can get to pay the bills."

"Sounds good," Tom said. "I'll close the file on the incident."

She expelled a contented sigh. "Maybe now, Jimmy and I can find some peace and settle into our new normal."

He rotated on the blanket, so that he faced her rather than the setting sun. "About that . . ."

Rachel chewed on the corner of her lip. Ever since she'd foolishly given him that impulsive kiss on the beach after he rescued Jimmy, she'd been waiting for him to let her down gently.

"I was kind of hoping," Tom went on.

She held her breath, bracing herself for disappointment.

He searched her eyes. "I'm hoping that I might be a part of yours and Jimmy's new life."

Excitement swelled in her chest, and Rachel grinned. "I'd like that very much."

"I don't mean just as a neighbor," Tom clarified.

She laughed. "I hope you don't kiss any of your other neighbors the way you kissed me on the beach yesterday."

He smiled. "I'm pretty sure that *you* kissed *me*."

Rachel knew she was grinning like an idiot, but she couldn't help herself. She leaned toward him, closing the gap between them. "Are you sure you want to be with someone so impulsive?"

Tom touched her cheek. "I've never been more certain of anything."

Like a wave crashing over the shore, fear suddenly swamped her, and she froze.

He edged back, obviously concerned. "What's wrong?"

Rachel blinked back a ridiculous surge of tears. "I'm a jinx. You need to know that. God's taken away every person I've ever loved, except for Jimmy."

"Are you saying you love me?"

Flustered by the idea, she stammered, "W-well, I guess you could say I might be falling in love with you."

Every last trace of concern vanished from his countenance. "You don't know how happy you've made me. I was so afraid you didn't feel the same way about me."

Rachel blinked. "But I'm a jinx. I've lost my parents, my husband,

and my in-laws." She swallowed a sob. "Yesterday I almost lost Jimmy."

"But you didn't. And you didn't lose me." Tom caught her hand and stroked his thumb across her fingers, studying them for a moment. "I know that it's hard to understand why loss and other horrible things happen to us."

She nodded, waiting for him to continue.

He drew a deep breath. "All my adult life I've avoided romantic entanglements because I didn't want to be the cause of that kind of emotional upheaval for someone else. But this weekend, I realized that we can't insulate ourselves from bad things. Bad things will happen sometimes. And I want to stand with you through the good and the bad."

Jimmy slid onto the beach blanket next to them, splattering them with sand. "Mommy, you're supposed to say, 'I do.'"

Too stunned to speak, Rachel gaped at her son.

"He's asking you to marry him," Jimmy explained. "I saw it on TV. Right, Tom?"

"Uh," Tom sputtered, then laughed. "I thought we might start with going on a few dates first."

Rachel laughed at the blush flooding Tom's cheeks. "I'd love to," she told him.

"Okay, now you kiss him," Jimmy instructed matter-of-factly.

"That's one smart boy you have." Tom leaned forward, then gently cupped her face in his hands and touched his lips to hers.

As if the entire island were rejoicing with her, the sun slipped into the water with an explosion of purple, blue, crimson, and gold, and everyone on the beach applauded.

Rachel knew that somehow everything would be all right.